T0197091

It Ends
then
It Begins

Glenda Y. Carter-Brown

authorHOUSE®

AuthorHouse™
1663 Liberty Drive
Bloomington, IN 47403
www.authorhouse.com
Phone: 1 (800) 839-8640

© 2018 Glenda Y. Carter-Brown. All rights reserved.

No part of this book may be reproduced, stored in a retrieval system, or transmitted by any means without the written permission of the author.

Published by AuthorHouse 06/14/2018

ISBN: 978-1-5462-2851-6 (sc)
ISBN: 978-1-5462-2850-9 (e)

Print information available on the last page.

Any people depicted in stock imagery provided by Getty Images are models, and such images are being used for illustrative purposes only. Certain stock imagery © Getty Images.

This book is printed on acid-free paper.

Because of the dynamic nature of the Internet, any web addresses or links contained in this book may have changed since publication and may no longer be valid. The views expressed in this work are solely those of the author and do not necessarily reflect the views of the publisher, and the publisher hereby disclaims any responsibility for them.

It Ends Then It Begins

"*Hello Elonda, what are you doing today?*" "*Well you know, the usual, it's 8:00 in the evening!*" "*Sara, why do you ask me this every day?*" "*I don't ask you every day, just Mondays!*"

"*I've been doing the same thing every Monday, since I was 18 years old and that hasn't changed!*" "*Oh, I thought maybe…*" "*Maybe what?*" "*I'll go to one of those stupid meetings with you. Then you go back to doing what you do after Monday is gone!*" *Elonda tells Sara.*

"*Elonda, you don't have to be real mean!*" "*Oh you are saying whole names 2 times. What's going on?*" "*Nothing I just, I just… I'll talk to you tomorrow, when I see you out there, bye.*" "*Wait what, don't hang up….*"

It was just too late. Sara hung up feeling lonely and alone. She needed someone to talk to because she was tired of her life and wanted it to change but didn't know how to go about doing that. So, she just got ready to go to church, a place she has no place in but seemed accepted for who she is, and no one seems to judge. But something was missing. She felt that there had to be more that meets the eye. She gets dressed in her best clothes. A dark blue pant suit with the jacket buckled down in the front. The blouse was a silk red-cranberry blouse that covered her neck, so the beauty of the suit could be seen, along with her.

Sara is a very pale, 25-year-old girl who has 2 friends, she knew she could always trust and be there for her. Sara the youngest. Shy, reserved, and loitering about when she needs to ask a question or make a statement.

Her hair is red, like fresh cherry Kool-Aid. Her eyes were the most beautiful green, like big glossy emeralds. Her lips were plump. Very beautiful girl, who didn't feel that way about herself. She's confident when she needs to be. But she likes to sit in the "cut" so to speak, so she won't be noticed, until Elonda comes around.

They've been knowing each other since Sara was 4 years of age. When they first met each other, they just stared at one another for a few minutes until the bell rang. They both walked to the school side by side as if no one else were there.

"What's your name?" "What's your name?" "I'm Sara McCormick. "Hi. I'm Elonda Richards." "Nice to meet you!" Sara said. "I'm 4 years old. You are?" "I'm 7!" Elonda said. "Why are you here?" Asked Elonda. "I'm waiting for my mom to come out from taking my sister in. Then we'll be leaving." "I knew you didn't go to this school." "Nope, too young." "Well, I have to go to my class. Are you coming back with your mom, to get your sister?" "Yes." Sara grabs Elonda's hand. They are still walking towards the door. "You mind if I call you La La for short?" Sara asks "Huh?" "Did you say La La? That sounds different. Yeah, you can." Only when it's you and me. "Pinkie promise?" Sara asks. The girls did a pinkie promise. Sara and her mom left. Elonda went to her classes.

Sara was so excited she met someone new and different like her and that the girl likes her. All day long she kept thinking about her meeting Elonda. She couldn't wait to go to school with her mom to get her sister.

But something happened. Mrs. McCormick had to go to school early to get Tracy. Sara's sister. Tracy got sick and couldn't stay at school all day. Sara was angry and sad. She was angry because she didn't get to see her new friend La La but sad that her sister got sick. Tracy is 10 years old. She was born sick. It took her mom 6 yrs. to be confident enough to have another child. You could tell Sara and Tracy were sisters. They both have those beautiful green eyes and red hair. Tracy's hair is more of a strawberry blonde. It looks blonde from a distance but red when up close. Both girls are very pretty.

They moved from London to the U.S.A., North Carolina (Charlotte), because their father got stationed in the U.S.A. 5 years ago before Sara was born. At first it was hard for the family to leave their home, of 10 years, to move to a totally new world, it seemed.

Even though Sara was born in the U.S., she still had the British accent and she loved it because she felt and seemed different. Tracy really missed home, her friends, and her school. She seemed to have been sick all the time since getting to the U.S. Tracy was not as pale as Sara. She had a few freckles and her skin was slightly tanned.

When Mrs. McCormick arrived at the school an ambulance was already there. Tracy was having a hard time breathing. They had to rush her to the hospital. Sara was confused. Some lady grabbed Sara by the hand and told her everything was going to be okay, but deep inside Sara knew it wasn't going to be alright…

Tracy screams," Where is my mum!? What's going on? I want my mum!" Ms. Loften, one of Tracy's teachers, said. "Here is you mother!" Ms. Loften said as she walks with the paramedics to the ambulance.

A whole day went by. Sara sat there waiting for her mom to come pick her up from Tracy's school. Sara finally goes to sleep. Sara slightly wakes up as her father picks her up. She hugs her father tight around his neck. "I miss you. Where is mom and Tracy?" "Just sleep baby." I'm going to take you home now." Sara goes back to sleep.

They finally get home. Sara's father puts her in her bed and she roll over balls up in the fetal position. "I love you daddy." He replies. "I love you very much." It seemed like Sara was sleeping forever. She wakes up hungry and with a lot of questions on her mind. "Are you hungry baby?" "Yes mum." "Here I have this for you." Mrs. McCormick gives Sara food and Sara just picks at the food until it is gone. In the meantime, her parents disappear to their room and Sara hears them whispering.

Sara was in the dark about everything and her questions were always ignored. Time seemed to have flown by.

What's Next

Sara is now 12yrs old. She is walking to school kicking rocks with her hands in her jacket pocket wondering what La La is doing because she hasn't seen her in 3 weeks and no one heard from her.

Sara is a good student, she completes her work get Cs, but Ms. Loften feels that she could do better if she focuses and quit day dreaming.

"Sara come here." says Ms. Loften. "This is a good story you wrote for your project, but something is missing." "What do you think it is?" At that time the bell rings and class were over, and Sara began to run out.

"Come back here Sara! I was talking to you! This conversation is not over! Now answer my question, what is missing?" Sara stood there starring at the paper in her hand that Ms. Loften gave her. "Um well here is the introduction, here is the body, 2 paragraphs, and wow the conclusion. All seems to be here to me". Says Sara. "Sara what is wrong with you! Don't you think I can see that! Okay you can go now!" Sara walks out the class with a mischievous grin on her face as she put her hands in her jacket pocket.

"That was crazy. I feel good that I dissed Ms. Loften. I've let her get away with telling me that I can do so much better for a long time. I shut her down. that puts a smile on my face. Man I got to go to church tonight I don't feel like it. I'm told that I always must do right, or else GOD will kill me.

Sara approach her house where her dad is on the computer looking at his emails and her mom in the kitchen getting dinner prepared for an early meal.

"Sara go wash your hands and come help me! "Ok mum I will." Sara runs to her room to put her books down and take her jacket off. "Hang that jacket up please Sara!" Sara paused, did a reverse walk to her room gets her jacket to hang it in the closet. Then she washes her hands, goes into the kitchen to start the tea.

"What you do in school today?" her dad asks her she drops the sugar bowl, it shatters as it hits the floor. "What you do that for girl!" I just asked you a question!" "Nothing dad sorry." She bends down to pick up the pieces. Before things got worse for her. "You need to confess your sins when you go to church tonight girl!" Mr. McCormick yells. "I am personally taking you to the front to the priest to get forgiveness for whatever you did!" "Yes Sir, I will!" She said that with tears in her eyes wondering where her sister is to save her as she always did.

"Come on Sara it's time to go! Please don't make us late again!" Mrs. McCormick yells up the. "Why do that girl loiter around when she knows what time Services start?" Asks Mr. McCormick. "Well honey maybe it could be the things you say and make her do at church." "What! Making her confess her sins in front of the congregation!" Don't you think that's a little too much honey?" "The bible does tell us not to irritate our children." Says Mrs. McCormick. "I never seen this as an irritation for her." "You know honey it could someday in the future discourage her from wanting to serve God." "Hum." he said as he opens the door to walk outside as Sara runs down the stairs.

Church was almost done, then it happened. Sara swallows nervously.

"Do anyone have anything to share with the congregation tonight?" The preacher asks. Sara was about to stand up then her father grabs her hand and pulls her down. She looks at him and sits down. Her father put his arms around her and say. "You are a good child. You have nothing to confess or be ashamed of." He kisses her on her forehead and she laid her head on his chest with tears rolling her face.

"Here I am 13 years old. I am a good girl but bored. I haven't seen Lala in 2 months She is 17 now. I've been used to seeing her since she was 10. I have been able to talk to her almost every day. I don't know where she is. That makes me sad. Here I am not knowing where my sister is and now Lala. What is going on! Is this what I must look forward to in my life! Nope I won't think that way!" Sara now reaches the school and she starts imaging how she will agitate Ms. Loften.

"I hate school it is boring! I've done all the work ahead for the week. I do it every week, now the teacher keeps picking on me telling me I need to be in high school instead of being in 8th grade. I would like to but I'm afraid I won't fit in and must be put back before I can go forward. I keep avoiding the issue. Ms. Loften said she won't talk to my parents about it until I give her the OK and that will never happen. I 've been a student of Ms. Loften since the 4th grade and what she doesn't know is I pretty much know what is next with her and I'm used to that but now if I skip 8th grade and go to high school she won't be there. I already won't have her next year. There must be a shortage of teachers in this school. Change is scary! Right now, I maybe bored but I'm safe and good." She laughs a little. "The year of is almost up anyway. If I put it off maybe the opportunity will pass me by. I have a few months to ignore the subject and then I'm 9th grade bound instead of 10th. Yeah!!!

Sara walks into Ms. Loften's class and sits at her desk. "I have visitors today to give you all some information about pursuing higher education. Mr. Murphey the Dean of the local Community College. Let's give him a warm welcome." Everybody claps for Mr. Murphey.

"Hello! How's everyone doing? I thank Ms. Loften for inviting me. We know the importance of furthering your education beyond High School. 35% of the students leave middle school to go to high school they don't know what they are going to do next. Ms. Loften and I came up with this program called "Lead Them Now". That program is to assist younger ones who have anxiety about going to high school never the less college. First, we're going to talk a little about the structure in high school, then branch over to College. You ready!" He laughs a bit. "Here is Elonda Richards to tell you about High School. "Hello! Again, my name is Elonda Richards. I'm in the 11th grade. Straight A student, Student Body President, Cheerleader, and other things that keep me busy and an eye on making thing endurable for the 9th graders so they won't give up before they begin. I've decided to be a part of this organization because it was hard for me as a 9th grader/freshman to the point I almost gave up. The point is I didn't and here I am looking at a full scholarship to any University or College of my choice. This is what high school is about. Of course studying for each class. You have like four classes on even days and three on odd days that seem like much. You also get study period or study group time. 20 minutes before class is over to give you a head start on your homework. The secret is take advantage of that time or you may get far behind. The classes themselves and the teachers are just like here in this school ready and willing to help. I know this school is set-up like High School as far as the different periods so you kind of know what I am talking about. I also know most of you have Ms. Loften more than others. I did too. She is a wonderful and caring Teacher. My point is, there are three more classes in High School than Jr High/Middle but just as you are doing well here, keep up the same routine in High School and study, study, study. Thank you for your time." The class claps as Elonda walks away. "Wasn't she great! All the organizations she is a part of she is still getting A's. I commend her!" Mr. Murphey claps for her. Elonda takes a bow and the class laughs. "See she got a sense of humor as well. Now for me to tell you about College still same set up only five classes on different days pretty much like Jr. High & High School. Just more advanced classed but at least you can have some what of the same consistent routine. Does anyone have any questions? No questions? OK. Thanks for your attention and I will hand it back to Ms. Loften."

"Well class. Let's give Mr. Murphey and Elonda a big hand to show our appreciation!" Everyone starts clapping. "Thank you again, Mr. Murphy and Elonda for coming out to speak to the students about High School and College."

They said in unison, "No problem, anytime."

Then the bell rings. Sara runs to catch up with Elonda. "Where have you been Lala?" I've been worried about you. "How things been going?" How does it feel being 17 now?" Asks Sara.

"It's too soon to tell. I'm sorry baby girl. I've been so busy as you heard to the point I feel so burned out. I don't mean to ignore you but I'm trying to keep my head above water!" "I'm sorry Lala. I didn't know. I don't mean to be selfish but, but... nothing." "Well Sara. I must get back to school now. I'll try to call you later."

Sara was happy. "Ok. We'll talk later then." "Good to see you Lala!" "You too baby girl!"

Elonda kept calling Sara for the past few days before she got too busy.

It was now April. Another semester has come, and Sara is still giving Ms. Loften the minimum work. C's.

"I figured since I'm going to 9th grade and will be in High School, at least one year, with Lala, I don't want to embarrass her with my C's. With her status, it would be much with me being a freshman. Never the less, with bad grades too! Maybe I want to be a part of an organization or something."

She walks home with a slight smile on her face and not a doubt in her mind that she could not accomplish it. She goes into the house. La La's parents are in the living room. Mr. Richard Mrs. Richards is standing together looking out the dining room window. Sara ignores what she sees and goes up to her room. She hangs her coat up, and slowly heads down the stairs.

What Happened

S ara hears whispering, so she tries to hear what they're saying, but they hear her coming down the stairs. The whispering stops. She walks in the room and with a weird smile on her face she asks. "Who died?" Both mothers looked at one another and says no one.

Mrs. Richards asks Sara. "When was the last time that you spoke to Elonda?" "I spoke to her just a few days ago. Two days to be exact. She told me that she wouldn't be able to call for a few days because she will be busy with school stuff." The last time I saw her, was at my school. She spoke to my class about how important school is and explained to me why she hasn't talked to me in a long time. That was two weeks ago. Why? What's going on? What's wrong with Lala?"

They both look at one another again and Mrs. Richards starts crying as Mrs. McCormick hugs her to comfort her.

Sara starts to cry too. "No, no, no not her". Then she runs outside, her father runs after her but could not catch her.

Mr. McCormick goes into the house. Everyone was standing there, in the foyer. "Where is Sara. Did you catch her? "No, that girl runs fast. She should be on somebody's track team. Man, she is fast. Aw, she'll be back. Don't worry, honey." Mr. McCormick says as he puts his arm around his wife. She buries her face in his chest and cries so hard that her husband remembered the last time she cried like that. He pulls her closer and tighter. He says in a soft voice. "She'll be back. She'll be back." He had a worried frown on his face. This was 4:00 pm when Sara ran away. It is beginning to get dark and Sara hadn't come back home. Her dad said, "Let me go look for her". He left and when he returned it was 11:00 pm with no Sara with him. "Where is Sara?" Mrs. McCormick asks, as she woke up. Mr. McCormick stood there with a blank look on his face like he was looking through his wife. Not a word came out of his mouth.

"Well, honey, did you find her!" Yells Mrs. McCormick.

"No! I looked everywhere and nothing!" I'm calling the police!" Yells Mr. McCormick. Mrs. McCormick jumps out of the bed to follow her husband to the phone.

"Hello, yes, I'm calling to report my daughter missing." "How long has she been missing?" "I don't know since about 4 pm this afternoon. Why!" "Well, sir I do apologize but a person has to be missing for over 12 hours before a missing persons' report can be made."

"Are you kidding me! She's 13 years old! For twelve hours!!! Are you crazy?"

"Wait, sir. I do understand your anguish! Calm down! I can help you better that way. Tell me what happened." Mr. McCormick told the 911 operator what had happened and the search for Sara started.

The time is now 2 midnight and no signs of Sara. By that time, a lot of neighbors had gathered at the McCormick's home to see what needs to be done. Everyone showed so much love and care at this time. Even people they barely knew. The Richards were there too because their girl hadn't been home for over 3 days. Sara didn't know. She assumed something worse, which lead to her running away.

The police come back to the McCormick's with a jacket in his hand.

"Is this your daughter's?" "No." Mrs. McCormick replies quickly.

"Wait that is my daughter's jacket!" Yells Mrs. Richards. "I bought that for her at the beginning of the year as a gift. She was doing so well in school." She grabs the jacket and holds it close to her, and broke down in tears. "Where did you find this jacket?" Asks Mr. Richards. My girl has been missing for over 3 days. And NOW you bring her jacket! Where did you find it?"

"In the park, by the bench, close to the ball field." "It still smells like her." Mr. Richards said as he tries to keep his composure. "Which means it has not been long, that the jacket was there!" Mr. Richards says loudly. "Take me there!" Mr. Richards demands.

"No, I can't sir. I need to have that area searched for the girls and more evidence. And I don't need you to go there tampering with anything that may mess up something that can enable us in finding either of the girls. Besides, we don't know if they are with each other. Mr. McCormick, I know something happened that caused Sara to run off, but Mr. Richards I don't know the details of Elonda's disappearance." Said Dt. Mitchell.

"That's just it. We all ate breakfast that morning before we all went our separate ways, as usual. Nothing seemed wrong. Now that I think about it, she did have a blank look on her face, but she still laughed at my jokes. She kissed us as usual, and we all went on our way." Mr. Richards looked at his wife as he said that. "Where is our baby and where did we go wrong!" He starts sobbing and his wife runs over to comfort him. He holds Elonda's jacket close to his face.

"I do apologize, but I must start the search team at the ball park, but please try not to go down there or tell anyone because we don't want the press or anyone on the possible crime scene. I will call you in two hours, with an update, whether something is found out or not. Please stay put." Dt. Mitchell said as he walked out the door with the officers.

Search for the Girls

It has been over four hours and Dt. Mitchell has not called the family to let them know and he didn't give a phone number or card where he can be reached.

"I'm going crazy! They haven't called and it has been well over 4 hours!"

"You're right Jim. It has. Maybe we should go to the park and see." Mr. McCormick says.

"Wait, guys! You shouldn't do that! Remember what Dt. Mitchell said. The less people down there, the less attention. We don't have one child missing, we have two. "Come on Jim and Tom! We can't risk things getting any worse!" Mrs. McCormick yells. "Ok! I understand! But if he doesn't call by morning. I'm going down there!"

"I agree Jim!" Tommie McCormick yelled.

The ladies look at each other and walks into the kitchen. "Anyone up for some coffee?" Asks Laura McCormick.

"Yeah! I'll take some!" The men say in unison as they go into the kitchen.

Then Laura bursts into tears saying. "What happened Tommie! What did we do wrong! We raised them to have faith in God's saving grace and now… look! We have lost our girls!"

She covers her face and Tommie runs over to hug and comfort his saddened wife. The Richards looks at one another. "GOD!" We see where that got them. "God! What does he have to do with this? Where is God now that our daughters are missing? Look at you are crying! You are asking the same as me. Where is God as we need Him now?" Jim says in a sarcastic tone.

"Honey! calm down! Just because Laura is crying that doesn't mean that she doesn't have faith in God. She is human and expressing grief. It is a common emotion. As for me. I feel so angry because I want my daughter safely with us! I'm sure that Lara feels the same way!"

"So, please! We are here to comfort one another not criticize and make matters worse!" Jim, please honey. Stay calm, and we'll get through this!" Lana Richards says as she rubbs Jim's shoulder.

"You are right Lana. I'm sorry Tom and Laura, for my out burst it's just… never mind. Forget it. I'm sorry." He grabs his jacket and starts to leave. "Jim! Where are you going!" As Tommie grabs his arm to stop him. Jim looks at Tommie angrily. Tommie did not let go of Jim's arm. "I know we all are going through a tough time right now, but we will get through this. Just like every other time! I'm glad you all are here with us to help one another because friends always need friends and we consider you both as being more than friends. Tommie said. "We all are family and our girls are the ones that brought us together. I know Jim. It's rough, but God has been the one who has helped me, and my wife get through all we've gone through with Tracy. Her being ill all the time and then dying. Sara has been going through a hard time with her now finding out why Tracy has not been around. Now with Elonda missing whom is like a big sister to her. That was what broke the camel's back. That's why we didn't tell Sara about Tracy dying. Exactly what we feared has happened. All we can do is pray and God will send them back to us!"

Jim puts his coat down and grins. "Tommie, you make good speeches. Why aren't you a preacher or something?"

"Well, Jim I thought about it many times, but I haven't found the best church or religion yet."

"I thought you were already going to a church."

"Well, we do because of what the bible says. We must associate with fellow believers, but I'm not 100% comfortable with where we are. I just stay put until I am presented with another opportunity."

"Hmm...To me that doesn't make sense! It's like you are staying at a job, in a relationship, and being some place that doesn't make you feel complete! It appears to me that you are not being true to yourself." Jim tells Tommie.

"I know I don't have a relationship with whomever I'm supposed to, but I know of the existence of a higher being but I just don't recognize that one who oversees my life. I feel that I have some say about how it goes. I know I don't have full control. Some things happen that are not my fault. Unfortunately, like what we are going through right now. I have a sense of contribution, if not control". "What you mean Jim? Tommie asks with a puzzled look. I mean if I have an accident in my car I think about how I contributed to it." Tom laughs. "Nothing because that is why it is called an accident not a deliberate." Both men laugh. "I never thought of it that way." Says Jim. "What do you mean by I am not being true to myself because I'm choosing to stay at a church that I am not fully comfortable with?" You see Tom it's just my point of view. We can't control some events that take place in our lives but I think we can control where we live, work, and worship. It is our God given right, free will, if I may say. Just like you chose to serve God. Don't you think he has a place where he exclusively wants to be served? I believe all religions don't have God's standards in mind so there must be a religion or organization/church that lives up to his standards in a certain pattern of life, worship, and even beliefs that he 100% accepts." I feel if that is what you desire then you should search for it not settle." Jim says. Let's take your family for an example it started with you choosing a wife. Did you settle for any woman or did you take your time and look for the right one?" "Um yeah I feel I could not have chosen anyone more suited for me." Tommie looks at Laura with a big smile on his face. "Right!" which ended up in the right balance of family too. When you found out that Tracy was sick did you settle for just the one doctor?" "No!" Do you get my point?" Jim asks Tommie with a smirk on his face. "If you aren't, comfortable with settling, then why would you settle with your service in life that is about God?" "Jim, you are talking a lot of good for someone who don't go to church all the time." Tom, I think I can serve God if I chose. I am not fully convinced of any God issue. I was saying all that because people settle too much as it were, for things that are so important to their happiness and it appears to me you would be happier if you knew where you wanted to worship and go to that place. As for me I am happy without that kind of thing, so my happiness is not in jeopardy." Jim says smiling with his head up with confidence.

The phone rings. Laura jumps up to answer the phone after one ring. "Hello!" "Yes, this is Dt. Mitchell. "Laura puts the speaker on. "Yes, we all are here!" "Well, we didn't find anything else. No finger prints nothing. I apologize for it taking longer than I expected but so far, we have nothing to give as a lead on any of the girls." Tommie interrupts. "What you are telling us is to do nothing and wait for you and your team to do all the work looking for OUR girls!" There's no way! I refuse to sit around any longer! It's still light outside! We'll do whatever is needed to get our girls back home! That's including press." "Ok Mr. McCormick! Ok! Me and my team will continue on our end." Dt. Mitchell hangs up.

Everyone looks at each other as Laura hangs the phone up. "Ok where do we go from here." Lana asks. "We need pictures, flyers, go to the school, ask questions, and go to the local news to get others involved."

"Ok Jim. Tommie says. "Let's go!" The families parted ways to gather all the information they need to get the search under way.

They all met back up at the Richard's home with the pictures of the girls on the flyers. They have separate flyers with 1 girl each. Then flyers with both girls. If anyone sees them separately or together they would know to contact either Family. They were putting flyers on the poles as they made their way to the schools. They walked instead of riding. They made it to Sara's school first spoke to the principal and the principal took them to Ms. Loften's class. "Hello, Mrs. Jackson how may I help you?" Ms. Loften asks.

These families have something to speak to you about." "Hi Ms. Loften." Tommie says. "Hello Mr. and Mrs. McCormick. Mr. and Mrs. Richards." "Can we speak to you for a minute in the hall?" Mrs. Jackson asks. "Yes sure!" "We have a problem we need you and your students to help with." Ms. Loften had a concerned look on her face as she moves in closer to the McCormicks. "The girls have been missing." Mrs. Jackson says. "I know you all will find your girls." She says as she hugs the mothers and shake the fathers hand. She leaves to go back to the office. "Sara ran away yesterday after school when she heard us talking about her sister Tracy's death as well as Elonda's disappearance. Elonda been missing 4 days now." Mr. McCormick says. Ms. Loften grabs her mouth with a gasping sound and say. "Oh, my goodness!" She walks into the class, only the McCormicks went in but the Richards stayed in the hall. "Class Mr. McCormick has something to ask you all." As he tries to hold back the tears he takes the flyers out and says. "Sara ran away last night. We need your help to find her. Not only her but Elonda Richards too. She has been missing 4 days now." They hand the flyers to Ms. Loften. "If you help us in looking for them as well as handing out the flyers to everyone, we would really appreciate it." The McCormicks proceeds to leave the class. Ms. Loften follows. "I will make sure the students get the flyers and I will help too." "Thank you. Ms. Loften, we appreciate it." Mrs. McCormick says.

Then she goes back into the class and closes the door. The class was very quiet and then one student raises his hand. "Yes Josh." "Well um…… nothing it is dumb never mind." "No Josh. What is it?" "I saw Elonda 2 days ago. When I was on my way to school, getting into a green car by the store. She didn't look so good." "Ok Josh thank you for being so brave in coming forward." I will call the Richards and inform them." "I thought nothing of it. I did think she didn't look so well." "What do you mean?" "I mean… I dunno I mean she didn't look the way she looked when she came here a few months ago. I mean she was dressed different. Her hair was different. I mean she looked like a street walker. I've been seeing her get in the same car before I even knew who she was but then she was looking fine nothing wrong. Then when she came up here I said to myself that's the same girl I see every morning for about 3 months. Getting into the same car at the same place about the same time. I was expecting to see her. I didn't mention anything about it because it was none of my business. I figured something was wrong when I haven't seen her in 2 days. The last time I saw her she looked so much different than the other times." "I'm sorry Ms. Loften I didn't know. I should have known something wasn't right!" "No honey, you did good Josh!" Class I'll be right back!" Ms. Loften runs to catch the McCormicks, but it was too late. She remembered what they said about Detective Mitchell. She calls him and then he conferences with the families for her to tell everyone what Josh said. "I want to speak to that boy! Mr. Richards says. "You can't do that! There are procedures for that! I will speak to him along with his parents." Dt. Mitchell blurts out. They all hangs up. Ms. Loften went back to her class and apologizes. The bell rings. Josh walks to her desk. "Am I in trouble?" "No honey! You did a great thing! Dt. Mitchell will get in touch with your parents and talk to you all more. Don't be afraid you did nothing wrong." She rubs his shoulder as they both walks out the class.

In the meantime, Sara's walking down the main street in the next city over where no one knows her. "What have I done? Here I am out of anger left home and I know my parents are worried sick. Why did I do that? How can I face everybody again? I wonder what happened to Lala. Why didn't they tell me about Tracy? It doesn't matter anyways I'm not going back. I can't take my parents treating me like a victim locking me up. But I sure am hungry and tired.

Questions Answered

D t. Mitchell went to Josh's house to meet with him and his parents. "Hello Mr. and Mrs. Jamison. I'm Dt. Mitchell and I come here to talk to your son Joshua about the Richards girl." "Ok, come in. Mr. Jamison says." Have a seat. Joshua come here. Dt. Mitchell is here to talk to you!"

Josh comes walking slowly and Dt. Mitchell sits down and patts the seat next to him for Josh to sit. Josh walks over there slowly to sit. "Don't be afraid. You are not in trouble. You did a good thing. Your parents should be proud of you." "We are!" Larry Jamison says.

"So, tell me what happened." Josh tells Dt. Mitchell everything he told Ms. Loften. "Tell me Joshua. "Please Sir, call me Josh." Ok, Josh Describe the clothes she had on for me?" "When?" All times I saw her!"

Dt. Mitchell chuckles and replies." The last time you saw her." "Oh. Ok. She had on a pink jacket with a light blue or purple looking stripe on her sleeves. A white blouse, blue jeans, and pink kicks on." "Ok, Josh. Is there anything else you can remember?" "Um, well… she seemed to look scared, sad, or something. She got into a car that was green. All this happened as the car took off in a hurry burning rubber like he was running, mad or something. I mean she has been doing this for sometimes. She also been dressing like a street walker, but that day was different. Her face didn't look good. She didn't have any makeup on. She just didn't look like the girl that came to the school or those other days I saw her. Am I in trouble?" He asks, as he looks at his parents.

All three of them said no in unison. Mr. Jamison said. "Son, that was a brave and honorable thing you did. Especially remembering the details."

"I have a confession to make." Josh says. "I like her. I looked forward to seeing her each day. Especially when she came to the school. I thought she was pretty and smart. I'm so sorry. I'm so sorry. I'm sorry!" Josh says while sobbing and holding his face in his hands. His parents look at each other. Dt. Mitchell looks at Josh's parents, as he pats him on his back. Josh's mother walks over to sit next to Josh. He puts his head on her chest and say." "Come on, Joshua, things will be fine," as she kisses his head with a concerned frown on her face. Mr. Jamison stands there with his arms folded with a frown on his face.

"Well, I think that is enough for now. I'll leave you people alone." Dt. Mitchell gets up puts on his hat then lets himself out. Mr. and Mrs. Jamison wait for Josh to stop crying.

"Son. I've never seen you act this way." Mrs. Jamison say to him with his head still on her chest.

Josh lifted his head to say. "Yes, mom I know." He sniffs and stifles his feelings. He gets up, puts his hand on his mother's shoulder and he walk to his room. Mr. and Mrs. Jamison look at each other as Mr. Jamison walks and sits next to his wife and grabs her hand. "I have never seen him like this before." "Me either." Mr. Jamison whispers. "What are we going to do, Larry?" "Well Carol, I guess we need to help look for the girl."

The next day Mr. Richards yells to his wife "Honey I got it!" When Jim peeps out the window he opens the door. "Hello how may I help you?" "How are you doing?" We're Larry and Carol Jamison our son Josh was the last to see your daughter and he showed us the flyer of her and another little girl." May we come in?" "Sure. Jim moves to the side to let them both in then led them to the living room. "Honey! "I'll be there in a moment!" "How are you and your wife been enduring?" "One day at a time Larry that's it." Lana walks in the room. "Honey, this is Larry and Carol Jamison. This is my wife Lana. Their son was the last to see Elonda. What is his name?" "Joshua." Lana gives Carol a hug and they all sit down. "Oh, excuse my manners!" Lana says. "Can I get you both some coffee?" "No, we are fine. We won't take long. We came to tell you that Dt. Mitchell spoke to Joshua and we decided that we want to assist in looking for your girl!" "Oh, thank you, but there are 2 girls missing. Ours and Sara McCormick. Her and Elonda are best friends." "I forgot honey to tell you, they know." Lana kept speaking. "Sara ran off when she heard us speaking about Elonda missing for a few days. There's no clue in them being found!" We can use all the help we can get. We already got flyers a reward for information, and the cops looking. They are more concerned about Sara because she is 13 but not much about Elonda because she is 17. They are saying she could have just left home. They found her jacket in the park over 3 days ago. Nothing is being done about it!" Lana says in a frustrating tone. Jim jumps up in a panic pacing back and forth from one end of the living room to another with an angry look on his face hitting his fist in his other hand. "I'm so angry! I don't know what to think or do! This is my only child! A beautiful and gifted child! There is nowhere I can think of to look for her! "Lana gets up runs to Jim grabs him and starts crying. Jim calms down a little to hold Lana close to him as he looks at the Jamisons. "The Jamisons looks at each other. "Well we have to go here is a check for whatever you need. More flyers, reward money, whatever just fill it out it is already signed." Mr. Jamison says. Jim refuses the check. "Thank you." We don't need your money we have money. Is this all you came by here for! To get us upset then leave!" "We have some where to go too like you do so take your check and leave!" "Wait a minute! Jim, I didn't mean it like that. When I saw Joshua break down because your daughter is missing we were compelled to help find her. This check is for now. We came by to tell you that my boy saw Elonda get into a car for 3 months at the same place at the same time and I wanted us to go sit there to see if she shows up even though he said she didn't come for two days before she was reported missing." The Richards grabs their coat and they all leaves. The Jamisons drove. Elonda never seen their car before so as hours went by Jim reluctantly say, "Um. Um Larry um I'm sorry for the way I treated you earlier." I'm just, you know." Larry interrupts Jim. "I understand says Larry. I understand! No apologies needed. I should have explained myself better before I presented the check. It's just me being a businessman. I can be so insensitive at times. I apologize as well." The women look at each other, grabs each other's hand and smiles as they sit in the back seat. "Is anyone hungry! Larry asks?" "Yes!" Everyone says at the same time. "Ok you all stay here, and I'll go in that store to get us sandwiches to eat and something to drink." Jim yells. "Just water!" "Me too!" The women say together. Larry goes into the Eatery to order the food and get the water. He goes to the cooler for the water. A girl sitting at the table with a guy looks out of place. Larry looks at them. The girl looks at him. Larry hurries out of the store runs to the car yelling. "I think Elonda is in that place!" He points to the Eatery. Mr. Richards jumps out of the car runs across the street. Cars were honking and dodging him. Elonda heard the noise, went to the window. She sees her father. Elonda runs out the store to jump in a green car just as Josh described and drove off fast before Jim could catch her. Jim falls to his knees. Cars were honking and people yelling at him to get out of the street. The rest of them runs to Jim to pull him off the ground. He went wild swinging and yelling. "My little girl! My little girl is gone! Why! Why! Why! Lana grabs him to hug him tight as they both sob while the Jamisons hold one another. They didn't say a word. People start getting out of their cars to see what is going on. The police pull up. Jim was in a state of shock not believing that his only child ran away from him. The police questions them "Get Dt. Mitchell over here now! Don't touch my husband! We are one of the families that our girls are missing and we just saw our girl She ran away from US! Get Dt. Jerry Mitchell here right now!!! Lana yells at the police officers. Lana gives one of them Dt. Mitchell's card where he could be reached.

After 15 minutes. The Detective makes it on site. Jim still was not talking. Larry tells the Detective what happened and why Jim is not talking. Dt. Mitchell calls for an ambulance to come check him out. They come. The streets were full of people watching to see what was going on and the police say. "There is nothing to see here, move along go ahead move it! move it!" The crowds slowly disappear. After the medics checked Jim they said he is okay, but he should go home and get some rest. Lana takes him by the arm and slowly walks Jim to the Jamisons' car. They all went back to the Richards' home in silence. They get to the house. Mrs. Richards opens the back door so her and her husband can get out. The Jamisons were about to get out too. Mrs. Richards said to them we'll be alright you don't have to come in. They close their door wait until the Richards got in the house and pulls off. Mr. Richards sits on the couch and starts crying profusely and Mrs. Richards didn't know what to do but sit there beside him with his head on her chest and her head on his head crying as well. He looks up and says. "Why does God hate us so much?" Mrs. Richards replies. "I don't know honey. I just don't know." They both were crying profusely.

On the way home Larry and Carol talks. "I don't know how I'll feel if that was Joshua." Says Carol. Larry nodded his head in agreement. Then the rest of the car ride they didn't talk. The radio was playing music. When they when they go into the house. Josh is on the couch waiting for them. "How did things go with Elonda's family?" "Not so well." Larry says. "What do you mean!" Josh quickly stands. "Sit down son. Sit down. Larry says in a calm low voice. He put his hand on his son's shoulder. "Well we saw her and before Jim could get to her, she jumped into that green car and sped off." Josh jumps up again and yells. "Oh No!" Larry says "Wait a minute son. Don't get upset. The truth is, Elonda doesn't want to be found or she would have not run.

For 3 years, everyday Josh and Mr. Richards went and sat where they saw Elonda and she never came there again.

Sara Smiles in Spirit

S ara finally found a place to eat and sleep. Since she speaks and carries herself well. No one ever asked her age. The next morning when she woke up she was fed and had to leave due to the rules of the place.

She walks around with her head down so no one would talk to her to question her. She comes to this place where a lot of homeless people gathers. Men women, young and old. She sits alone so she wouldn't be noticed. A girl comes up to her holding out her hand to Sara. Sara looks up at the girl to say; "What do you want? I don't have anything." Leave her alone." The girl tells her; "I'm here to be friend you. Because you have been spotted by some of the people that don't care for anyone or anything. I've been out here for a long time, so they know me."

The girl extends her hand out again to Sara. This time Sara grabs it. The girl pulls her up and they walk away. They walk silently until they were not around the rest of the people. Sara asks her; "So what is your angle? Everyone wants something. How may I help you?" The girl starts laughing? "Girl are you serious! You don't know huh?" Your parents have a reward for any information on your whereabouts. If I want anything, I can have it. $25,000 just for you! That tells everyone who sees their posters that you are worth more than $25,000. Do you know what people like that will do for that kind a money! My suggestion to you is to go home to save your parents that $25,000. More than that, save them from all that heartache! I don't want anything from you! I'm giving you something and it is for free. That is information. Use it and go home little girl! People around here charge for information. That's the way things are these days!" Sara asks her. "What is your name?" The girl tells Sara. "Now I have to charge you for that!" Sara has a look of concern as she reaches into her pockets. "Um, um, um. I don't have any money, but I have this orange." The girl takes the orange and said; "I'm kidding. Call me Spirit. You are Sara McCormick. I like your accent. By the way, where is it from?"

"I don't have an accent. I am from here, the USA. My parents and sister are from London, England." "Oh, Okay," I see. Spirit says as she raises her left eyebrow. "What are you gonna do?" "I dun no." Sara says. They start walking in silence. Spirit and Sara hung out for a while. Suddenly, one day while they were hanging out Sara starts crying. "What's wrong?" Asks Spirit. "Why you cryin?" "Well, the reason why I ran away is my sister. I found out she died when I was 4. My parents kept telling me she was away to get better because she was real sick. The same day she died, I met my best friend Elonda. I call her Lala. The last time I saw her was when she came to my school. We talked on the phone. One day when I was coming down the stairs, I heard my parents talking, that's how I found out about my sister and Lala missing. Instead of asking, I ran out the door and my father couldn't catch me. I understand my sister is with God, is Lala too?"

Spirit sat there with her mouth open and eyes bucked. "Oh wow!" She says after a few seconds. "Oh wow!" she said again. "You mean to tell me you ran away from home because of what you might or might not heard? Are you crazy!" Spirit pulls out a cell phone. "Call your parents right now!" Sara asks; "You have a cell phone!" Spirit says; "You're asking the wrong question! You should be asking if you can use it!" Sara replies; "No, I will not call them!" Spirit yells. "If you don't volunteer to call them, I will and get paid to do it!" Sara says; "You go ahead." After you get the money, we can get some place to stay, instead of being out here!" "Are you serious Sara! You want to steal money from your parents through me! You won't have a home to go to! What do you like about being homeless?" "Well, nothing really. I just like hanging out with you.

If I go home, I won't ever see you again. Then, I've lost again! "If you haven't noticed, I'm not the happiest and the easiest person to get to know. I've always had Lala and now she's gone. She the only one who I had to talk to! Sara starts crying again, this time harder. All I have now is you! I don't want to leave unless you come with me!" "I can't do that Sara. That's your home!" Sara snatches the phone from Spirit's hand and dials her home number. Mrs. McCormick picks up. "Hello." Sara didn't say anything. She closes the phone. Mrs. McCormick calls back. Spirit answers the phone. Mrs. McCormick is yelling. "Who is this! Who is this!". Spirit gives it to Sara. She refuses to take it. In the meantime, Mrs. McCormick calls her husband to the phone, in a panic. He yells. "My family has been through enough already! If this is about my Sara, please say something!" He starts sobbing. Sara feels sick to her stomach to hear her father cry, she never heard her father cry before. She says in a soft voice. "It's been a year and a half. (her voice begins to get louder) You hung posters instead of looking for me yourself!" Mr. McCormick tells Sara. Is that you!" "It's not Tracy! Unless she has come back to life. Mr. McCormick is silent. "Sara! We're sorry we didn't tell you. You were too young you wouldn't have understood." "Well dad, I'm not 4 anymore. I understand a lot of things, except why you and mom did not tell me about Tracy! Then decided that I didn't need to know that my best friend, my sister, Elonda had been missing for a few days! You are sorry! I'm sorry I called!" Sara slams the phone close. Her face was now as red as her hair. Spirit says. "Girl, you're a spit fire! Calm down! So, now what?" Spirit asks as she tries to put the ringing phone in her pocket. Sara snatches the phone out of her hand before she puts it in her pocket. She answers it. "Don't call me anymore!"

"Sara, I know you're angry but…" Sara hangs up and this time took the battery out of the phone and put it in her pocket. Spirit didn't say anything for quite some time. She was a little disturbed and didn't want to make things worse. "With the battery out, they can't trace my whereabouts." Sara says. Spirit still didn't say anything. It was getting dark and they were getting hungry. Spirit told Sara to sit still and she will be back. Sara knew she was going to get them food and shelter. She did as Spirit told her. As always when it came to the same time, each day since the third day of Sara's presence. "Here Sara." Spirit hands Sara her food. "Come on. We need to get inside before it gets too late. Got your number?" "Yeah, here it is. You got yours?"

Spirit looks at Sara as they walk to the bus to take them to where they to sleep, every night. Spirit never sleeps by Sara. She would talk until Sara falls asleep. Spirit would leave. When Sara gets up, Spirit is nowhere to be found. "Come on! Get dressed! The bus is leaving soon! We can't miss it. I am in no mood to walk. You must have been tired. You fell asleep while I was still talking." "I know. "I guess the conversation I had with my father took a lot out of me." "Speaking of that, may I have my battery back?"

"Oh, yeah. Sorry. I meant to give it back to you last night. I guess I feel asleep." Sara gives Spirit her phone battery. Spirit puts it in the phone, as they get on the bus to get breakfast and hang out for the day. The bus driver yells. "Don't lose your ticket or you won't be able to get on the bus later for shelter!" Sara checks her pocket. "Got it" She didn't bother to ask Spirit because she don't want to get that look from her. She knows Spirit keeps up with her number. "Dang, the phone is dead!" "Now what?" Asks Sara. Spirit reaches in her backpack and takes out a charger. It'll be charged in ten minutes." "What is that! How did you do that?" "Don't get so excited Sara. I charge this every night, for moments like this. So, I can have phone service everywhere I go without of risk getting it stolen. Quit trippin' girl! Come on." Sara follows Spirit with no questions to go get their first meal of the day. "You want this apple Sara?" "You're not supposed to take food from here." Spirit grabs two and puts them in her backpack. "What are you going to do? Snitch on me and have us both without food and shelter tonight?" "Naw girl. I'm jus sayin." Spirit grabs Sara by the hand. "Come on. Let's get outta here." "Ok, I'm comin." Spirit and Sara start walking around. It is noon time. "I'm hungry. Can we get somethin to eat?" We are too far from the place that has lunch." "Here! I knew taking these apples was right. Eat this and sit here. I'll be back." Spirit leaves for what seem like hours.

"I should leave. I know she left me. Like everyone else has. My parents never left me. They lied to me, though. I wonder if I should call them back and give them a chance to explain themselves." Spirit was standing there trying to give Sara food. "Sara! Sara are you okay! Where did you go?" "Nowhere, I've been here all the time!" "No girl! Where did you go in your head?"

"Oh, oh. I was thinking about leaving because you took a long time. I thought you left me, like Lala and Tracy. I thought that maybe I should give my parents a chance to explain themselves." "So, you thought I was going to just leave you here? When I have been here for almost two years?" Sara grabs the food from Spirit. She also hands Sara the cell phone. "Let me eat first please. I need a straight mind to speak to them." Spirit puts the phone in the front pocket of her jeans. The girls find a spot in the grass to eat their lunch. Sara never thought about how Spirit comes up with everything she needs. She just accepts her kindness without question, thinking I'll pay later.

Home Bound

"**H**ello mum. Sorry about yesterday."
"Sara are you ok?" Mrs. McCormick calls her husband to the phone. He snatches the phone from Laura and say. "Girl do you know how crazy we have been? You have a lot of confessing and reporting to do. You have been disobedient." The phone was on speaker. Sara starts to hang up, but Spirit shook her head no. "Just listen." she whispered.

"Who is that in the background telling you to listen? Who is that?" Spirit grabs the phone from Sara to say. "Hello. I'm Spirit." "Spirit who!" Tommie yells. Spirit looks at Sara to say. "Wow, I see why you left." Tommie said. "So, you're the one who encouraged my daughter to leave her home?"

"No, I'm not. I found her and befriended her." "So, I guess you're looking for the reward money?"

"No! Did I mention it?" Spirit says loudly. "If anything, you should be saying thank you for looking out for your daughter, for almost two years! She is still a minor and a lot of people saw the poster you put up. She thinks no one knows her since she's never been to this city. People are hungry out here. $25,000 is not child's play. She has been with me all this time. I left her many times. If I wanted the money, I would have claimed it by now. When I had the chance! So, man you got issues. Is the mother around?" Mrs. McCormick takes the phone. "I'm so sorry about that and thank you. I hope to see you soon. Matter of fact, I demand to see you to thank you in person. May I speak to Sara?" Spirit replies." "Your welcome and sure." She gives the phone to Sara. "Sara!

Are you okay! I miss you! Are you coming home soon? We all miss you, including your father. You know how he is. I apologize if he hurt you." "Naw mum. I'm okay. Are you okay?"

"Yes. Now that I hear your voice! Do you need us to come pick you up?" "I don't know. I don't want to leave Spirit out here alone." "I'm good girl. I'm never alone. I always have someone who has my back." "Would you come with me anyways? I won't go home unless you come with me!" "Okay baby. Okay baby. I'm sure that it's alright if you come home. I love you dearly. My baby, my red head Cardinal. I forgot about that name you call me." Sara looks at Spirit with a serious face and asks. "Are you going?" There was a long silence. "Sara, Sara are you still there?" "Yes mum. I'm still here, just seeing is Spirit is coming with." "Give Spirit the phone." Sara does as her mother tells her. Spirit refuses. Sara pushes the phone at her again. Sara starts to motion that she was going to hang up. Spirit quickly grabs the phone. "Yes. How may I help you Mrs. McCormick?" "Well as you know, my baby won't come home unless you accompany her. So, please, I'm begging you. I don't care how long you stay, if my baby is in my arms again. I'll even give you the money too. Please help bring my baby home to me." "Okay, okay you don't need to beg. I want her to come home anyways. I'll stay for a few days but as for the money, you can donate it." "Donate it where?" "I'll tell you when we get there. You don't have to come here, we'll come to you." Sara yells. How!" "We'll be there in 2 hours." Spirit closes the phone.

Spirit tells Sara to stay put and not to move. "Here we go again. You're leaving me? How long you gonna to be this time?" "Sara calm down. I haven't left you by now and I told your mother I'm bringing you home and that's what I'm gonna to do! Sit still and don't worry so much." Spirit looks back to smile at Sara. "Well, at least I'm not hungry anymore."

A man walks up to Sara and starts to talk to her. "Hey sweet mama. How you doing? Wait! You that girl on the poster, aint cha?" "What are you talkin bout?" He calls his friends over. Pull that paper out!" He did. The man snatches it from him. "Yes, you are! See! See! Ain't she guys!" Sara gets scared because one of the boys with them grabs her by the arm. Sara pulls away from him and starts to run but a cab pulls up just as she was going around the corner. "Sara! Sara! What are you doing! I told you to wait for me! What happened!" Sara jumps into the cab, hugs Spirit, and said while sobbing." Four guys noticed me from the poster two of them grabbed me. So, I ran. I didn't care where I was. I just didn't want them to get a hold of me." Spirit rubs her head and say. "Shh, shh. You are fine, nothing happened. You are safe now." They went by the four guys. Sara points "There they are!" They see Sara pointing at them, but they didn't see Spirit. "I know who they are. They are homeless too." Sara looks at Spirit. "Wait a minute! How did you get this cab?" "Aw, Sara. You ask too many questions. Sit back and enjoy the ride." Sara starts talking as she looks out of the cab window. "I don't know what to say to them. It's been over 15 minutes and I don't know anything, maybe things have changed. so much to the point I rather be out here than there, especially if my dad is still a religious fanatic." She laughs, and she looks at Spirit. She gives Sara a bland "Ha-ha" like she was in another world. "Are you okay Spirit?" Spirit looks at her. "I'm okay. Are you?" "No. I'm nervous. I don't want to go back to the same stuff. I'm older now and different. Being out here has changed me. I feel so different now." "Sara is that a good thing or a bad thing?" "I don't know. I just don't wanna be lied to anymore by nobody! Lies do nothing but hurt and make people loose trust." Sara goes back to looking out the window. Spirit looks at Sara for a few seconds. Then they both were quiet and looking out their windows. The ride seemed to have taken forever. Then, they pull up to Sara's home. "Well, here we are." "Yes, we are." Spirit replies. Mrs. McCormick runs to the cab. But no one gets out. Then, Mr. McCormick comes out of the house.

"Are you ready, Sara?" "Take a deep breath and relax." Spirit opens the door to get out one side and Sara opens the other door to get out, onto the street. Sara's mother runs around the cab to grab Sara to get out the street. Where Spirit is. She hugs them both, as they walk into the house. The cab pulls off. Sara looks back "No one paid him!" "He was paid in full!" Spirit says.

Settling In

"Tell me Spirit. Is that your real name or a nickname? What do you do for a living? What is your reason for being with my daughter?" asks Mr. McCormick. Spirit put her fork down and looks at Mr. McCormick and said," I don't know you well enough to give you any information about me. As far as your daughter is concerned, if I had bad intentions towards her would we both be sitting here in this fine home of yours eating like a big happy family? The question is what intentions did you have for putting all these posters up, offering all that money for her safe return? You ask yourself, what are my intentions of being here with your daughter?" Spirit gets up from the table and proceeds to walk towards the door as she gets on her phone to call a taxi. "Why did you do that?" Sara asks her father as she ran after Spirit. She grabs the phone out of her hand and say. "Please don't go! Please don't go!" Spirit looks at her and say," I can't stay here! I'm not wanted! Something isn't right! I have to go!"

"I'm going too then. I can't stay here if you are not with me. I won't! I can't!" Then, Mrs. McCormick ran to Sara and Spirit. "Girls please don't go. Spirit you are welcome here. My husband has always been protective. Please don't go!" Mrs. McCormick says as she grabs Spirit around the neck. Then, whispers in her ear." I wouldn't know what to do if I lost my last child. Please listen to me. I want you here. You could stay as long as you want." Mr. McCormick comes to the foyer entrance and says. "Are we eating out here or what?" Then he tells Spirit to calm down. "I'm not accusing you of anything. I need to know who is in my house. So, calm down and come sit at the dining room table so we can eat this good food that Helena cooked for us to welcome Sara back home as well as you Spirit. Mr. McCormick smiles as they all walk into the dining room to eat. Mr. McCormick smile left abruptly as they all walked pass him with his hand out as to usher them into the living room. Spirit looks at Sara to tell her. "One mo time I'm gone… just one mo time. I'm gone and never looking back." She shakes Sara off from hanging on her arm. Mrs. McCormick says as she looks back at her husband. "We can't have that, now can we?" Mr. McCormick puts an evasive smile on his face as he throws his arms in the air as to say I surrender. Mrs. McCormick grabs both girls by the arm as they were walking through the living room to get to the dining room she smiles at them to kiss them both on the side of their heads.

It was silent as they all ate due to the tension in the room. "How's the food!" Asks Mrs. McCormick. Sara says; It is good, missed good home cooked meals. Spirit says; "Good." She keeps eating. Tommie says nothing. "Are you all ready for dessert?" Helena asks. "It's your favorite Sara, Chocolate Fudge Cream cake." Sara say; "No thank you. "She excuses herself from the table. Mr. McCormick yells. "Where do you think, you're going young lady! Sit and have some dessert!" Helena and your mum went through all this trouble to make sure you are comfortable, so sit right now!" Laura says; "Please Tom let her go!" Spirit gets up to catch up with Sara. "Where are you girls going?" Laura asks. Sara say; "I'm going to my room, it has been a long day and I'm tired." Laura gets up to show Spirit where her room is. "Come on Spirit let me show you where you are sleeping." "I have two beds!" yells Sara. "I want her to sleep in the room with me!" "Ok sweetheart." "I'll bring the linen to you. Your bed is ready Sara you don't need a change of linen. They both sits on Sara's bed waiting for Laura to come back. "Girl this bed feels good." Sara says. "You think so?" Spirit asks. "It beats the floor and old cots any day!" "I'm so happy that you are here Spirit, I don't think I could be here all alone with them." Laura was about to walk into the room, but she waits at the door to listen to more. "I understand why you left due to the secrets. It looks like you have a good thing going on here. "If you say so, all this time I believed them about what they told me about my sister and how they were going to see her. I had to go to school, so I never questioned them. I feel so betrayed. "I almost forgot about Tracy when Lala and I got close. I feel like I want to leave." "Your father he's a piece of work!" They both start laughing. "Your mom is really Kool and it seems she'd do anything to keep you here." I'm a stranger she knows nothing about me." "I know very little or close to nothing about you too. I do know this, if it wasn't for you…" I feel like God is giving me another chance at having a big sister. When you leave take me with you!" "I don't know Sara." Laura walks into the room just before the conversation went left. "Here you are Spirit." I want to thank you so much for convincing my baby to come home." "Mum I am not a baby anymore!" Blurts out Sara. Spirit looks at Sara with a frown on her face. "Thank you, Mrs. McCormick, for your hospitality. I'm so grateful and happy that you are here Spirit." "Ya'll have a good night, by the way Spirit you can stay if you want. This is your home too." Laura says as she smiles and closes the door behind her. Laura stands in the hall holding her hand over her mouth to keep the girls from hearing her crying out of joy and confusion. Tommie comes and grabs her by the waist to guide her to the other side of the house. They stood by Tracy's door and Laura starts crying even harder. Tommie grabs her head to put it on his chest with tears rolling down his face feeling his wife's pain.

"It's going to be alright honey, it's gone be alright" Tommie says as he rubs his wife's back gently to comfort her. They walk into their bedroom. "I don't recognize Sara anymore Tom, she has changed so much. She is not my baby anymore, she even told me that." More tears start running down her face in disappointment. "She need to beg God to forgive her!" Come on Laura let's get ready for bed." Laura snatches away from Tommie to run into the bathroom. She slams the door. Her crying turns into loud sobbing. "I'm sorry sweet heart, I'm so sorry!" Tommie says as he put his hand on the door knob to go in, but he stands there with his head down then he walks away.

The next morning Sara comes down the stairs rubbing her eyes and stretching her arms. She looks around as she made her way to the kitchen. "Good morning sleepy head." "Hay mum." "You hungry?" "I don't know." Sara says as she looks around. "What you want to eat baby? Sara looks at her mother with a frown on her face. "I mean sweet heart." Laura corrects herself. "I said I dun no!" "Honey you seem lost what's going on?" "Umm where is Spirit?" Sara asks as she looks towards her mother. "She said. She had to leave. She said that she is coming back before dinner." "Oh NO!" Sara yells. "Why didn't anyone wake me up!" She ran out the door to run away. She stops in her tracks as she sees Spirit sitting on the steps. "Sara what's wrong! "Where are you running to?" Her mother asks as she runs behind her. Spirit turns around to look up at the commotion. Spirit stands up and say. "Hey what cha doin. Sara why so in a hurry?" Sara slowly walks towards Spirit. Laura stands there to see what was going to happen next. "Why are you acting like that Sara!" Screeches Spirit. Sara just sits where she stopped before getting to Spirit. She then puts her hands over her face because she was crying uncontrollably. Spirit rolls her eyes as she walks up the stairs to sit by Sara. Laura with a worried look on her face stands at a distance to see what is going on. "What's goin on Sara?" "I-I thought you had left me!" "Sara, you do know that one day I am leavin, right?" "I will let you know when that time comes." "OK" Spirit says. They both gets up. to go in the house, by that time Laura had walked into the kitchen. "Is everything alright?" "Yes." Sara says. "You promise Spirit?" "Yes, Sara I promise. Have I ever not kept my word?" Spirit asks her as she looks down at her. "Well no, it always took you so long to come back so I thought…" Spirit interrupts her to say; "Business sometimes don't have a time line." "I'm here now RED!" They both starts laughing. Mrs. McCormick can I assist you in getting the lunch dun?" "What it is lunch time?" Yells Sara. "Yup. You've already slept half yo life away." Laughs Spirit. Laura starts laughing too. "The bed was nice and soft. I forgot about that." Sara says with embarrassment as she goes over to kiss Laura. "Thank you, mum." Laura kisses her back as she tries to hold the tears back. "You're welcome dear." "Am I goin to help with the food or what?" Spirit asks with her hands on her hips. "Helena already got things ready, all we have to do is fix our plates and dig in." "Ok, then. Well I'm washing dishes. I have to earn my keep around here somehow." "Don't worry about that Spirit our housekeeper does all that." "When did we get a housekeeper?" Sara asks. "After you left things was hard around here, I needed some help as your father puts it." They sit down to eat.

After lunch Laura asks Spirit to come so they could talk alone. They went to the back porch to sit. Spirit stands there as Laura sits. "Spirit you said that I can donate the money to a Charity of your choosing. You still feel that way?" "Yes, I do." It is called 'Help Someone Foundation.' Spirit says. "Oh Ok." Laura says as she starts writing the check. She repeats the name of the Charity. Laura hands the check to Spirit as she stands up to hug Spirit. "I am ever so grateful to you and always will be indebted to you for taking care of my little girl and bringing her home safely after all these years". Spirit stood back as Laura leaned forward to hug her. "No problem." Spirit said as she walks back into the house.

"What are you girls going to do today?" Asks Laura. Spirit says; I should go back over there. I have some mo business to attend to. "I'll be back later. Tell me Mrs. McCormick what is too late?" "Midnight." "Ok". Spirit says as she walks towards the door. "I'm going to!" yells Sara. "I'm goin by myself, you just got home. You been gone for about 2 years. I think you and your mother has a lot to talk about. You told her thank you earlier, show her how thankful you are by spending time with your parents. I'm sure you've got questions as do yo parents." Sara looks at Spirit disappear as she closes the door. Sara stood there in the foyer looking lost and sad with her hands in her pockets. Laura comes to put her arm around Sara's waist. "Sara come sit with me in the family room." Sara reluctantly went with Laura. "I want to get to know you again Sara. I missed so much time with you." Sara sits there looking the other way like her mother wasn't in the room with her. "Tell me about your experiences for all the time you were gone." Sara turns to look at Laura. Her face as red as her hair. "My experiences!" "My anger for you and dad made me not want to come home. I still would not be here if Spirit wouldn't have talked me into it!" Sara got up. runs to her room and slams the door. Laura sat there stunned with tears in her eyes.

Tom walks through the door, hung his hat and coat on the hall closet. He walks into the Livingroom and Laura tried to hide her tears and pain of what just happened. "Hey honey, what is going on?" I thought I heard a door slam. Laura wipes her face as she stands up to go hung Tommie. "Nothing Tom. How was your day?" "Not as eventful as yours." Tommie says as he hugs his wife. "Are your hungry honey?" "Yes. What did Helena stir up for us today?" I gave her the night off because I wanted to cook but..." Well how bout we go out to eat. What about that?" "You choose the restaurant dear." "Where is Sara and that girl?" "You mean Spirit." "Whatever." "I'm not hungry. Since you don't want me to cook. You're hungry, you go out by yourself." Laura says as she slowly walks up the stairs. Tommie walks behind her as he watches her go around the corner. "Ok honey, I'll just see if there are any leftovers, or I'll order in!" He shouts up the stairs.

He goes to the fridge to see if there is anything in there to eat or make quickly. He slams the fridge door and yells. "Where is Helena!" No one answers him. "Oh, boy here we go again. "It seems she was sad when Sara left, now she seems even sadder since she came back. I don't know if I could handle this. I must be strong. It is not the time to jump ship. Maybe I should drown when this ship sinks." He says under his breathe with laughter. What can I do to make things better? Maybe I should take off from the business for a while and try to endure that strange girl. She did bring my 'Cherry Top' home to me even though she is not a little girl anymore. Tommie thought as he stood at the kitchen counter looking at the ceiling. He slowly walks pass the living room to the stairs standing there like he is about to go fight a monster and must prepare a strategy for his attack. Tommie gets to him and his wife's room and slowly closes the door as he looks up at the ceiling, thinking. "Please God let me be able to handle what is coming next."

"Honey are you feeling well? You stormed out, did I say something wrong? Please talk to me!" "You said our daughter should be begging God to forgive her. With that attitude, I think it should be you begging for forgiveness!" "What you mean Laura! I've watched you for the past 2 or so years crying, sleeping, fighting me, and staying up all times of the night looking out the window for that selfish little girl! Now that she's back, it seems all was beginning to be a little less stressful now things are more stressful than before! You're attacking me as if I've done something wrong! I've been here through all your crazy! Can I please get a little credit for the peace that was here in this house!" "Tom! How dare you turn all this on me! You're the one who always made her confess sins that only you could see. When was the last time you hugged her or even told her that you're happy, glad, or maybe relieved that she is home safe in one peace? Spirit whom you always call 'that girl'! We don't even know what she had to give up making sure our daughter was safe out there! The thought of my baby, our last one gone! I couldn't have bared that!" Laura start crying profusely so Tommie sits next to her to grab her ever so close as if he was trying to put her inside of him for them to truly become one. "Honey I'm so, sorry. Please forgive me. I never thought of things that way. I am truly sorry; would you please forgive me?" Tommie starts crying too. Please forgive me?" I never want you to see me as a heartless monster. You haven't talked to me about your feelings in the past year or so. Now I was happy that you started expressing yourself to me again. Please don't shut me out Laura. I don't know if I can stand strong enough again through this not knowing what to do for you. I love you so very much. I know I don't say it often, but I figured you knew." Tommie whispers to let Laura know that he is sincere.

They hear a door close. Tommie jumps up walks quickly to the door. It was Spirit coming into the house heading up the stairs. Tommie quickly closes the door before she sees him.

Spirit walks into Sara's room to her crying. Spirit puts down her things on her bed and asks Sara; "Why she crying? "I've never seen you cry so much. What now?" Spirit asks in an irritating way. "I heard them arguing about me." "What you mean by that?" Sara rolls over on her stomach to bury her face in her pillow wailing so her parents wouldn't hear her. Tommie knocks on the door. "Come in" Spirit said. Tommie walks in to see what was going on. "Sara what's going on? Why are you crying?" Tommie grabs her to pull her onto his lap the way you do a baby. He lays her head on his chest. "Oh, my beautiful Cherry Top. I know I have not shown you much attention and I know how dishonest we were in not telling you about Tracy. I thought it would be better that way. I was wrong. Now I don't know how to deal with the pain I caused you and your mum. You both are the most important persons in my life. I couldn't bare it if I lost you again even forever. Please forgive me for being less of a father and more of a mad man who think I know how God want things. Spirit come over here." Tom says as he looks her way with his hand held out to her welcoming her to come over. "Excuse me, Mr. McCormick may I ask you what you want?" "I want to apologize to you too. For not expressing my gratitude for you keeping my Cherry Top safe out there. I have been un-hospitable towards you. My wife is happy with you being here and now I understand fully why. Thank you Spirit too for being a person of your word and here still making sure Sara is settled in at home. I can't thank you enough." "You are welcome Mr. McCormick. I know you are a protector and you were doing just that. I am a stranger and you know nothing about me. I understand. I'm a big girl I've seen more than you can imagine. Ya'll good people a lil thowed off but good people." Spirit says without accepting his invite to come over close to him and Sara. Tom kisses Sara on the head. Laura walks in. "I guess this is a family reunion." Spirit was thinking as she made her way out the room to the kitchen. She poured her some water and went to the back porch.

Spirit Breaks Loose

It's been six months now. Things appears to be calming down. Laura is not as sad anymore since Sara been home. The family has been communicating well, resolving things going forward. Sara realizes how blessed she is and being a part of a family.

"Sara what are you up to this day?" Asks Laura. "Huh mum pardon." Sara looks toward the living room as she was coming down the stairs heading for the door. "Mum would you say it again, I didn't hear you." Spirit and Sara was laughing and talking to each other. They both stops and goes into the living room where Laura is. "I asked, what are you doing today?" "Oh, I dunno whateva Spirit wants to do." Sara turns to look at Spirit. "What are we doing?" Spirit looks at Laura. Mrs. McCormick what do you think all of us should do?" "Well Spirit, it's been six months we all been doing things together. I would love to spend time with my daughter." "Ok" Spirit says, as she walks out the door. "Where you goin!" yells Sara. Spirit didn't answer she gave them a smile as she walks out the door. She disappears around the corner before Laura and Sara have a chance to see her off.

"Sara let's go to the park." "Yes, that's a good idea. Let me change first, so I can beat you running!" They start laughing Sara runs up the stairs to change. While Sara was changing, Laura was standing at the foot of the stairs thinking about. How rough it's been. I think I got my baby back. "Look mum, I can still wear my outfit like yours!" Laura looks down at her outfit then back at Sara's. They both bursts out laughing. Sara asks; "Do you remember buying these for us?" "Yes, dear you look great in it. Laura tries not to cry, instead she takes off running. Sara comes running down the stairs behind her. "Wait for me mum!" "Come on slow poke! Catchup if you can!" Laura yell and laughs. Sara catches up with Laura. They jog to the park. When they get there Sara looks over at the school. She just stands there. Her head starts spinning as she starts thinking about how her and Lala met. How her sister was sick. Wondering why her mother took her to school in the first place. Everything hit her all at once. Her head was spinning so much that she feels like she's on a merry go round. She drops to the ground without notice. "I'll bat I can beat you to the bench Sara." Lara starts running faster when she reaches the bench she sits. "Aha I beat you!" Laura notices that Sara was not there with her. She looks at Sara on the ground. A crowd was beginning to gather around. Sara wakes up and starts kicking and screaming "Get away from me! Get away from me! Mum, Mum!" Lara runs faster than she has in a long time. "Move, move! This is my daughter. Sara, Sara!" "Mum, mum!" Sara hits her mother very hard in the face. Sara starts crying and apologizing to her mother. "Don't worry about it baby mum is here. Let's get you home." During their walk home Sara apologizes again. "You got a hand on you!" Laura says as she tries to laugh but couldn't because her face hurts. "I'm so sorry Mum, it's just... I started thinking about the past 9 years of my life, when I looked over at the school I got light headed." "Do you want to share what you were feeling?" Sara looks over at Laura. "I see you learned some things from dad huh?" They both laughs. "Without your father's help through all this. I might have wasted away from a broken heart." "Mum that night I ran away I felt my whole world being pulled right from under me. I couldn't handle it. I hated school. Dad riding me about God. Where was God when Tracy died! Why has he not brought Lala home!" Sara tries very hard not to cry. Laura hugs Sara ever so close as they walk home. "I did miss home, but I didn't want to be there anymore. I felt like a stranger in my own life. I felt so lost! I was always upset, sarcastic, and unappreciative. Not caring how you or dad felt and your love for me Especially letting Spirit stay. I know it hasn't been easy for you in the past two and a half years. I...I felt all alone. Spirit gave me hope. She really took care of me out there." "I know baby.

I am forever indebted to her for that. Bringing you home safely." "Did you give the reward money?" Sara asks as she looks at her mother. "Yes, she donated it to a Charity of her choice. She said she wanted it to be confidential, but I checked and the Charity she chose exists." They got closer to the house hugging one another around the waist. "I'm gone go call Spirit to see where she at!" Sara starts running, her mother as well. "You don't have to call her because here she is, waiting for us!" They run to Spirit and there was a group hug, but Spirit broke away abruptly. "What's wrong Spirit?" Sara asks with a concerned frown on her face. "Is everything alright?" Spirit asks the same question of Laura after seeing that bruise on her face. Spirit didn't answer Sara. "Yes, Spirit all is well now." Laura says as they walk into the house. "We had fun! Mum has some power in those long legs, she left me in the dust!" Sara laughs. Laura and Spirit starts to laugh too.

"Are ya'll hungry?" Spirit asks. Me and Elena cooked dinner for everyone. "Yes! I'm starving. What ya'll cooked?" Sara asks excitedly as she jogs into the kitchen to investigate. "You need to go and get freshened up and so do I." Laura and Sara run up the stairs giggling like best friends. Sara goes into her room. Laura jogs to hers.

Laura sits on the bed for a few minutes thinking. That was scary Sara fainting like that. I'm so glad she's alright and she told me what was going on when that happened. I got a souvenir to keep for that trip as she tries to open her mouth wide. Laura held her jaw. "Man, that hurts! I never been hit like this before. How am I going to explain this to Tom how this happened? She gets up to head for the bathroom. There was a light knock at the door. "Yes, who's there?" "It is me mum. Can I come in?" "Of course, you can darling! Laura says with excitement. "Mum I am a little afraid that Spirit is going to leave now that things are fine between me and you." "Awe baby don't worry about that! I'm sure things are fine with Spirit. By the way will it be so bad if she did decide to leave?" "Well umm... I dunno. I haven't thought about it. Sara says with her head down sweeping the floor with her foot. "Honey it's going to be alright. Let's go down stairs to see what Spirit and Elena prepared for us. I'm famished! Aren't you Sara?" Laura asks as she leaves the bathroom.

Tommie walks in the house as Laura and Sara was coming down the stairs. "Hey Honey!" Laura says.

"Hey dad!" Sara yells as she runs pass her parents as they kiss their hellos. "Um, what's smelling so good?" I got home just in time, a home cooked meal!" Tommie says as he rubs his hands together while running up the stairs. "I'll be down in a minute! Don't start without me!"

Tommie runs again into the dining room. Everyone was eating. He stopped in his tracks and says.

"Who am I here!" I went almost two years with her depression, anger, lack of sleep, and not eating. I won't think about the stuff I was experiencing. Quite some time now I've been putting myself last! All I asked was not to start without me, so I can say grace!!" Everyone looks at Tommie in shock. "Honey come sit down." Laura says as she holds her hand out presenting the chair to Tommie. Tommie reluctantly sits down as Laura requested. All looks well." This don't look like something Elena would cook!" Tommie says as he tucks the napkin in his shirt collar. "You right." Elena says as she brings Tommie his drink. "Thank you. Elena." Laura did you cook?" "No Honey Spirit did with Elena's guidance." "What Tommie yells as he Slams his napkin down and walks out the dining room to the patio talking to himself. "I've tried to accept this stranger in my home, supporting her Charity with my money, sleeping in my house night after night. Who is she? Now she's cooking in my kitchen!" I'm simply tired of all this she has to go!" Tommie walks back into the dining room where they all are still eating and laughing." "Honey are you ready for dessert?" Laura asks. Spirit baked this delicious Chocolate Fudge Cream Cake; almost better than me I must admit." Then she starts laughing. Tommie stood there with his arms folded staring with an angry frown on his face. "You're ignoring me huh? You didn't see me get up and storm outside?" "Um yes dear, is everything alright?" "I see that bruise on your face! Were you ever going to tell me what happened!" "Oh, this thing, we'll talk about that later." "What else have you been keeping from me?" "Tommie sits down. "You haven't touched your food." Laura says. "I'm not hungry! Elena didn't cook this food!" I don't trust her! When I was thanking her the other night she ignored my hand of gratitude. Now she's cooking! I haven't felt comfortable since she been here!" TOM!! her name is Spirit and she is showing her gratitude the best she knows how! I think this is a great way to show it!" "We still don't know anything about her! Have you even tried to ask anything about her? It's been long enough! We know nothing about her!" "Tom what do you need to know?"

TOM her name is Spirit and she is showing her gratitude the best she knows how. I think this is a great way to show it!" "We still don't know anything about her. Have you even tried to ask anything about her? It's been six months and we know nothing about her!" "Tom what do you need to know! OK, how about this, you count what we know compared to what we need to know! One, she got our daughter back home safely. Two, she protected and provided for her all the time she was gone even when Sara didn't even want to come home. Three, she didn't want the reward money she gave it to ones that are less fortunate than us. Should I go on Sweetheart!"

Sara sat there in shock. Spirit slowly stood up from the table and said. "That's okay, this was a farewell dinner anyways. I'm leavin cause my time has come and my work here is done." My friend needs me to come back to…. Never mind. Spirit goes to get her bags out the foyer closet. Sara walks into the foyer as if she was in a trans. "Sara you're about to be 17 soon, it's time to stand on your own. Besides, I'm not wanted here." Laura runs up to Spirit to give her a hug Spirit dodges out of her way. "Spirit you are wanted here!" Laura starts to cry. "Please don't go Spirit you are wanted here. It is almost like I got my two girls again. Please don't go!" Laura pleas. "You make me so happy." "No! I think you both are happy because I stayed to keep Sara from leavin." Laura stops crying, looks at Spirit with anger. "Leave then, just go!" While pointing to the door. Sara was still in shock not able to say a word. Spirit leaves. Sara runs after her after a few seconds. By that time, Spirit was around the corner all that's left is her shadow. Sara comes back into the house yelling. "See what you did see what you did!" She runs up the stairs to her room and slams her door. Laura stands there looking at Tommie with a blank look on her face. "What just happened here?" Laura runs up the stairs. "Honey everything will be alright wait and see." Laura tries to open the door but it's locked. "Let her lone she needs to get used to being without that girl!" Tommie yells up the stairs to Laura. Tommie goes back into the kitchen throwing his hands back in the wave. "Forget it." Laura was still at Sara's bedroom door crying shaking her head.

A Heart Is Found

Spirit went back to the shelter. She went into the main office to sit. She had a frown on her face. Thinking about Sara. Wondering is she ok. "Awe what's wrong?" When did you start the sentimental thing?" Spirit looks at her friend and says; "I feel so bad for that girl. Her mom is a great mother, caring, and understanding. I think Sara finally realizes it. Her father is a very hypocritical man. He said he is a Christian which is fine with me, but he often said some dumb stuff! Well that's him over there! I'm not the one to judge. He's messed up!" "We all are messed up in some kinda way." "Yeah I hear ya!" "Tell me something Spirit. What made this girl so special?" She didn't belong around here. She was nothing but a little baby to me. She knew nothing of the homeless life and refused to go home. I felt it was my duty to keep her safe. I did! Like others in the past. Many have come and gone. I never gotten this close to any of them like Sara. Some knew about the streets. They love them. Because of the freedom they think they have. There are some that think they know it all. They don't need my help. Some have left their homes because they didn't want to follow their parents' rules. If they didn't listen to their parents, who am I to them, they should take directions? I won't have the patience to deal with them. Don't get me wrong, I'm not gone let any of them get treated any kinda way. I'm not gone hold their hands either." Now that's the Spirrit I know. Again, what about this Sara girl, having a nonchalant demeanor, what makes her special?" "Let me see hum, she was 13 years old, she never mixed in, she stuck out like a sore thumb. She reminds me of myself at that age, feisty and all." They started laughing. Ok girl I get where you comin from. Before

I got here. I was in her shoes. You know that." "Yeah." Spirrit says. "I left home and never looked back." Gennie says. "I'm stable now, with rewarding work. I can't complain. My education has done well for me. I do miss this little girl I met when I was younger." As Gennie kept talking Spirit mind starts to wonder to her past as a little girl. "Did you hear me Spirit!" "Huh what you say?" "I was saying, I had my whole life mapped out. Where I want to live, what kind of man I want to marry, how many kids I want to have. Then it seemed that my whole life fell apart in an instant." Gennie said with tears in her eyes. "Well Spirit." Gennie says while wiping her eyes. "What's next Who you gone rescue now?" Spirit looks at Gennie in a sarcastic way. Spirit got up and said. "I dun no. I'm thinking about taking a hiatus from all this!"

She says as she waves her arms around with a frown on her face. Gennie stood there speechless because she was not expecting that response. "Ohh!! Ummm!! Gennie says after a few seconds of silence. "What's that supposed to mean!" Spirit yells. "Calm down Spirit!" says Gennie with her hands out in front of her with a concerned look on her face. "To be hard, you surely are emotional. All this must have taken a toll on you. Going back and forth from here to there especially at night. If you feel you really need a break, please take one because you look like you are in a lot of pain right now. Is there anything I can do?" Spirit just sat there with her head in her hands and elbows on her lap. She looks up at Gennie. "I dun no." I'm goin to my spot and sleep, if I can." "Okay." Says Gennie. Spirit stood up to walk by Gennie as she walks by Gennie put her hand on her shoulder. "I'm gone be aw rite don't worry bout me says Spirit as she disappears out the door. Gennie yells, "I'mma pray for ya tonight!" Then went back to doing her work.

Spirit takes a deep breath as she walks to her spot. When she gets closer to it she stops and says. "Forget this, I don't want to! I'm gone disappear for a while. I can't! This too much!" Spirit looks at the bag in her hand then walks away. She didn't go home. "I'll call Gennie to let her know where I'm at." "Gennie, I'm outta here." Gennie heard a lot of noise in the background. "Spirit where you at?" An Airport?" You sure you wanna do this? You haven't flown since… Spirit interrupts her and say. "I got this! I'm good! I just need to help myself after this last girl scout mission." I need to face some obstacles I've been avoiding for 5 years now. We talk later." Spirit hangs up the phone and looks around to see where she must go to catch her flight. She throws the back pack on her shoulder and walks toward the gate. Gennie calls her back. "You jus gone hang up on me?" "Sorry girl my mind is going a hundred miles per hour." "Talk to me!" Gennie says. There were a few seconds of silence. "I feel unsure about my sanity and my well-being. Helping Sara was good. I was beginning to feel like I belonged. Like a family. I knew it was time to go when Sara's mom looked at me and said I want to spend time with my daughter alone without me!

That's when I came to see you. You were already gone. I walked back to Sara's house, as I was walking I saw them running, laughing, and playing. I Kept walking to the house. When I got there, I asked Elena to help me cook a special dinner for the family, but she had already done that. I asked her was dessert made. She let me make Sara's favorite cake. Then I went to sit on the porch they walked up all hugging. I felt sad. I realized no matter how I helped people and try not to get attached… I have to face my fears." "Flight 323 is about to board at gate 5. You have ten minutes!" An announcement comes over the loud speaker in the Airport. "Well Gennie that's my flight. Gotta go. Take care of yourself. It's my time now. I'll be back soon. Give me a lil time. I'm hurting, lonely, and lost." "Okay Spirit we talk later. Take care of you now." Spirit hangs up the phone.

The walk to the gate seem like the longest walk ever. Spirit was already there waiting to board the plane. She takes a deep breath as she walks down the corridor that leads to the plane. She starts sweating and her head was swimming. She thought to herself. "Stop panicking." You've been through things way worse than this. I must do this. I may not get any more chances to face my fears." She boards the plane, sits down in her seat with a relieving deep breath. "So far so good." She says to herself. A man comes to cross over her to get to his seat. He leans over and ask. "Would you please trade seats with me? I don't too much care for the window seat." Spirrit abruptly says. "NO! Thank you. I'm fine where I'm at." She closes her eyes to meditate. The man stops looking at her to look out the window at the baggers loading the plane.

The plane got closer to its destination and a little turbulence shook the plane. Spirit opened her eyes sat up straight as she held onto her seat. "Everyone calm down!" said the flight attendant. "It's just a little turbulence as we approach our destination. "Please put on your seat belts to prepare for landing." An announcement was made. "Hope you all enjoyed the flight, sorry about the bump. Welcome all to San Juan, Puerto Rico. Thank you for riding Flight 323." Spirit hasn't been home in years. She goes outside walks up to one of the cabs. "¿Donde va la Señorita bonita?" Spirit gets in the cab and says. "Calle de 23. Por favor." "Señorita, you speak English?" "I prefer it." Spirit tells him. He drives her to 23rd street. She pays him. He says in Spanish; "¡Ten cuidado ahora, que es peligroso aquí para una chica guapa como usted!"

"Soy de aquí." Spirit says. "I'll be careful." She says as she disappears into the building.

The Confrontation

S pirit took a deep breath as she put her key in the door hoping it works. It has been over 3 years since she used that key. She unlocks the door with a sigh of relief. She walks in slowly and quietly. The three-people sitting on the couch looks at her. They all runs to her to hug and kiss her. Then another person comes out to see what was going on. He stood there with his arms stretched wide not saying a word. Everybody moves aside. She drops her back pack runs to him they hug as Spirit starts crying." Abuelo, Abuelo", (Spirit calls her grandfather) "¡Yo soy aquí! ¡Yo soy aquí!" She hugs him so hard until he turns red. The woman comes to grab her arms from around his neck and says "You're gonna kill him Mija, let your grandfather go!" Spirit lets him go and apologizes to her grandfather several times."

¡Mija! You've been gone for so long I'm glad you come home! I thought you was never coming back here after what happened." Her grandmother nudges him on the arm and say. "Not now honey. Let her get in to rest. Are you hungry Samantha?" "Abuela I don't go by that name anymore. It's Spirit." "Oh, ¿Espirita?" "In English grandma, please." "Ok ok Spirit." Spirit and her grandmother starts laughing. Spirit gives Bela a big kiss and she says. Yes Bela, I'm starving. ¡Puedo comer un caballo!" "A horse huh?" "Well you may be close. How about a cow instead?" Everybody starts laughing. "Go wash up Sam... I mean Spirit." Bela says with a smile on her face. "Gonna take some time to get used to Mija." Spirit does as her grandmother say. While in the bathroom the children put her bags away. "Gracias Abuela it was delicioso." Spirit gets up from the table and to start the dishes. "I see things haven't changed. Spirit go sit, relax. You must be tired form that long trip. Joey, Maribel, come clean the kitchen!" Shouts grandmother. "OK! Bela here we come!" "Well Bela I'm going to lie down, can we talk tomorrow, please?" Spirit asks.

The next day Spirit rises before everyone. She goes onto the balcony to look at the sun rise and to listen to all the street noise going on below. She shuts her eyes to listen. Bela comes and taps Spirit on the shoulder. Spirit jumps "You scared me Bela!" She says as she grabs her head. "Sorry Mija. I didn't mean to scare you." She says as she hugs Spirit as they go into the house. "What do you all want to eat?" Spirit asks. "It's already done. The babies will warm it in the microwave. I have to go to the doctor with your grandfather this morning." "Is everything a rite?" Spirit asks with a concerned look on her face. "Oh, it is nothing but a yearly checkup." "I'll stay here with the twins then." "No need that has already been taken care of. We didn't know you were coming." "Oh, oh that's okay, I just want to help that's all." "You're fine Bela says as she grabs and caresses Spirit's face. "Okay Bela. I'll find something to do." Spirit gets a call right before she finishes her sentence. "Hey Spirit, how ya doin'?" "Good but feeling like an intruder. "What cha mean?" "I wanted to come home because I miss it and my family. What are you doing?" "I'm on my way to my geology class. I hate it! But I know this is what Lala and my sister would want. I been outa school for so long, it's hard to go back." "Good!" Spirit says. "Well I'm at my class now. I pray things get better." "I have to make it better! I'm kool though, you enjoy your class, we talk later or tomorrow." "Okay love you Spirit." "I adore you Sara, bye." Spirit hangs up the phone. "What am I doing?" Spirit stands there as if she was meditating on her actions. "There is no place for me here." She says with a trimmer in her voice. Then there was a knock at the door. Spirit yells. "¡Un momento por favor!" She runs to open the door. "Oh, it's you." she says as she walks away with a frown on her face. She was thinking. "I'm outa place."

"¡Hola! ¿Como esta? Spirit's brother asks. "Fine!" She says in a nonchalant voice. "Well, well, well. I see you have given up speaking Spanish huh.

Since you've been in the big city?" "Shut up Manny! I see you haven't changed." "Yes, I have! I'm only doing my big brother thing. Come give me a hug! "¡Mí hermana pequeña!" "¡Ya no soy poco!" "I come and go as I please!" Spirit says with a smile as she runs to give Manny a big hug. "No, I haven't forgot my Spanish. I didn't speak it that much where I was." "Okay let's see. "¿Dónde has estado?" "¿En los Estados?" "¡Por qué!"

"I know that. Which one or ones? Maybe I can come visit you there." "As you see I'm in this city. Who said I am going back to the states!" Manny starts laughing as he looks around. "Where is Bela y Belo? The twins too?" "She took Belo to the doctor... Manny interrupts. "What! What's, wrong with Abuelo!?" "Nothing it's his yearly checkup! You crazy! If you would have let me finish you would have known that!" "Um, he says as he looks around. "They left you here by ya sef?" Spirit looks at Manny with her head tilted to the side with a smirk and frown on her face. Manny starts laughing again. "Why you lookin like that?" "Boy I'm not that person anymore." Spirit said calmly. "Yeah, right, whateva." Manny said. Spirit leaves to the kitchen. Manny follows her. "I gotta keep an eye on you." "You do that. Do you want something to eat? I'm bout ta fix me sumthin." "Naw sis." She looks in the fridge, as she was about to ask Manny again he was gone. She goes in the Livingroom to see where Manny went. He left. She shakes her head as she was walking back into the kitchen. The door opens, in comes Belo and Bela.

"¿Que pasó en el médico?" "Todo está bien." "¡Bien bien!" Spirit says. "Come here Samantha!" Belo yells. "Spirit goes to sit by Belo. He pats her on the knee and she grab his hand to hold it with a smile. "What's going on Belo?" There was silence in the room. "Nada, solo quiero hablar contigo. Dime a Mija. ¿Lo que has estado haciendo tan importante que te mantuvo lejos de casa?" Spirit's phone rings. She gets up to go to the balcony. It was Gennie. "Hey, Spirit, how things goin?" "Girl it's fine. I'm sittin here talking to Belo." "Who's that?" "That's my grandfather." He just asked me what I was doing that was more important that I didn't come home. I don't know what to tell him." Are you a shamed of what you were doing here?" They were silent. "No! I don't think they would understand. That I've been homeless the whole time I've been there." "Girl you crazy! I'm gone let you deal wit that. While talking to your grandfather it may help you get a prospective on things. Okay we'll talk later girl." Gennie hangs up and Spirit puts her phone in her back pocket as she walks in the Livingroom to sit next to Belo. "Estoy en buena salud para ser un anciano." She laughs. "Belo, you look like you're in great health. An old man I don't know about that." They both laughs. "Don't try to change the subject, ¡Mija!" What you been doing?" Why did it take you so long for you to come home? Just for a visit?" Spirit was thinking about how she could explain what she been doing in the States. She couldn't. She starts with the last question about visiting. "Belo, you remember what was going on before I left, don't you?" "Yes, I'm not senile!"

"I… I'm not saying that Belo. I just don't want to go through that pain anymore." Have you spoken to anyone in the States about what you have been through?" "What you mean, a shrink?" Spirit asks with a look of disgust on her face. Belo laughs. "Well yes, or anyone you trust." "No, I haven't." She said with a look of disappointment on her face because it is hard for Spirit to open herself up to anyone, including Gennie. "Well Mija you can tell me how you feel about being back after being gone for all those years." "It feels safe, you and Bela always made me feel safe. Gracias Belo." She said as she gives him a big kiss on the cheek. "Ah, de nada Mija. I'm happy that you didn't forget your Spanish. Well Samantha, I'm very tired, I'm going to my room. It's been a long day." Spirit's grandfather walks away he looks back at her and say. "I'm here when you want to talk." "Thank you, Belo. Buenas noches. "¡Te amo Belo!"

"También te amo." Spirit sits there alone drinking her tea, thinking how happy she is to be home. Maribel and Joey run over and jumps in Spirit's lap. "Hey Sam!" Joey says. She gave him a stern look. "Only Belo and Bela can get away with calling me Samantha no one else!" "Okay

Spirit." They both say in unison. "It's time for bed twins!" "Aw, it's still early!" they sigh. Spirit laughs. "I see ya'll still speak in unison." She pats their little behinds as she took them to their room. "Sam... I mean Spirit, would you read to us like you used to?" Joey asks her as she was closing their door. Joey already had the book in his hands. She walks in backwards, sits on Joey's bed and takes the book. "You still have this book?" "Yup!" They said in unison. We will never get rid of this book, mom gave it to us." Maribel said. Spirit starts reading the book, within five minutes they were sound asleep. Spirit takes the book to the couch (her bed). She looks at the book. Tears fills her eyes. She starts thinking back ten years ago.

The twins were just born. She left Puerto Rico five years after that at the age of 22. "Samantha come here!" "Yes mom!" "I need your help!" "Okay, here I come. Spirit skips to her mom's room. "Girl aren't you too old to be skipping?" Spirit stops tilts her head. "No mommy." They both laughs. "Come closer yells Marisol. Spirit gets closer. "Tuck the pillows under me so that I can sit up. These babies got the nerve to wanna eat at the same time." Marisol held her hand out for Spirit to pull her forward to put the pillows behind her. "Hand me Joey please." Spirit picks up Joey slowing like he was going to break. "¡Dame ese chico! ¡No se ha ido a romper!" They laugh as Spirit takes Joey to her mom. "Mommy it's good to see you laughing again. I miss That." Marisol took Joey from Spirit and said. "Me too." Maribel was already feeding. In a sarcastic way, Marisol said. "Let the party begin." Spirit watch for a few minutes thinking how happy and beautiful Marisol looks with those babies.

Marisol had Manny and Spirit at an early age. She was 17 when she had Emanuel Jr. Spirit came 2 years later. The twins came 17 years later. Marisol died 6 months after having the twins. Spirit had a hard time dealing with that. Manny Sr. got really depressed and Manny Jr. stayed gone most of the time, that's how he dealt with Marisol's death. It was hard for Manny Sr. to connect with the twins. That's when Marisol parents came to take over. They never found out why Marisol died. That made things more frustrating for everyone.

Before this took place, Marisol was not able to take care of the twins. She was always tired and sleeping. She wasn't getting better, going back and forth to doctors, hospitals, clinics, and emergency rooms. Marisol didn't want Spirrit to worry and spend all her time taking care of her and the twins. Her parents volunteered to come to ease the load so that Manny Sr. could work and continue to take care of his family.

On day, the twins were crying like crazy Emanuel Senior had not gotten in from work as usual. Spirrit went in there rubbing her eyes from sleep. She stood there in shock, she could not scream out for help nor move. Instead of calling someone, Spirit went and laid next to her mother. She let the twins cry never consoling them. Spirrit pretended that Marisol was sleeping not saying a word. Spirit felt like a part of her died with her mother. As if no spirit was left in her. That's how she got her name.

Belo and Bela came in the room yelling.

¿Que está pasando? ¡Ah Dios mío! ¡Sam, ven aquí!

¡Algo está mal! ¡Ven rápido! ¡Ven rápido!

¡Llama al 911 ahora Sam! Belo went to call 911. Spirit was still lying on her mother. ¡Ven aquí Samantha! Marie went to pull Spirit off Marisol but she would not let her. Manny Jr. came in, he started yelling and screaming No! ¡No! ¡No! ¡Mamá! ¡Mamá!" Belo said, "¡Necesito su ayuda Manuel!" "¡Consiga a los bebés!" yelled Bela. Manny Jr. Grabbed the twins then took them in the Livingroom. Manny Sr. was whistling as he walked into the house with flowers in his hand, he was anxious to see Marisol and the twins. Marisol was allergic to most flowers, so this was a special occasion. He stopped whistling because of all the noise, he dropped the flowers, and everything ran into his and his wife's room as Bela was trying to pull Spirit off Marisol. By this time the ambulance had arrived the workers ran pass Manny Sr. The emergency workers started yelling at Spirit and Bela. ¡Mueva salir del camino, ahora! Manny Sr. Grabbed Spirit quickly so they could work on Marisol. Manny Sr.

was held Spirit to keep her from going back over there to her mother. He looked up at Bela asked, "What happened? Spirit was struggling and wiggling trying to get out of her father's arms until he held her tighter. She grabbed her father around the neck crying and yelling ¡Mamá! ¡Mamá! ¡Mamá! Bela told Manny Sr. ¡No sé! She kept saying to keep from breaking down herself. Sam held out his arms and walked towards Marie as he said softly, "Ven a mi cariño. Ven aquí." Marie slammed into her husband's arms as the emergency personnel said.

"Lo siento. No hay nada más que podamos hacer." Marie cried profusely. Spirit left out her father's arms as he knelt face down crying loudly. She walked behind the 911workers as they left the room. She walked as if sleep walking and sat next to Manny Jr. and took Maribel out of Manny's arms. Spirit sat there starring at Maribel. Everything got silent she no longer could hear the noise. She felt numb as if she had no life in her. No feelings, no fear, nothing. Like Samantha had left the building. Suddenly she came to, no one was there but her and the babies crying as if they knew something was wrong. She held Maribel closer and picked up Joey. She started crying with the babies. She said to herself. "What am I going to do now that mom is gone?"

Spirit was wakened by the twins. "Get up sleepy head!" Joey asks; "Were you having a dream or something?" Spirit rubs her eyes with a stretch. "What time is it?" She asks. "Almost 9 in the morning." Maribel says. "Dad was here, he kissed you on the forehead and went to bed." "Well, be quiet then." She says as she walks over to the door and knocks on it. "Come in Mija, it's unlocked." Manny Sr. Says; "I didn't want to wake you." He slaps the bed for her to come sit next to him. Manny Sr. grabs her to give her a hug and kiss on her forehead. Spirit starts crying as if her mother died again. Manny Sr. rubs her hair and says; "Oh, my little Samantha, go ahead and cry. He held her tight to let her know that he is there for her. She seemed to have cried forever. She looks up at her father and says; "Por favor, perdóname Papá." Manny Sr. held her tight without a Word but smiles at her with a tear Rolling down his face. "I couldn't stay here any longer. I just couldn't. Mommy made me promise not to tell anyone where I got the money. I miss her but I'm angry too. She left me to deal with all this alone." "She didn't leave you to deal with it alone. She left a letter concerning the money she left. You didn't have to let everybody think that you stole it." Manny said that I shouldn't have come back because of that." "Don't listen to him! You know how he feels about you leaving." "He didn't make it easy for me either. For five years, he made me feel like everything was my fault. I didn't know mommy was going to die!" She starts to cry again. Manny Sr. pulls her face up by her cheeks for her to look at him. "Bebé vamos a necesitar un barco si no dejas de llorar." They both start laughing. "Papi, are you mad at me?" "No sweet heart! I knew six months after your mother passed, you were leaving soon. I saw the pain you struggled with about your mother passing away. Your light went dim your spirit was slowly weakened. I knew it was a matter of time." "Did you get my letter saying good bye?" "Yes, the money too." "Why are you still working?" "If I don't, then what am I supposed to do?" "I don't know Popi. I don't know." She held her head down again as if to cry. She asks; "Do Belo and Bela knows about the money?" "They have a suspicion but never said anything about it." Joey starts knocking on the door. He came in and Spirit put a pillow over her face, so he wouldn't see that she had been crying. Joey runs to jump in his father's arms. Manny Sr. catches him as he gave Joey a big kiss on his cheek and Joey returns the kiss with the horn noise. Joey jumps out his father's arms runs pass Spirit as they both heads out the room. "See you later my little Spirit. I'm happy you're home!" Spirit smiles at him. "¡Te amo muy mucho Papi!" "¡Tambien te amo Mijita!"

When Spirit walks out the room her phone rings. "Hello Spirit, how you doin'? I miss you! I'm about to go to college and I have all these college applications to fill out. I need your help!" "I can do that. Let me get my brother and sister together. I'll call you back." Spirit closes her phone realizing what she said to Sara. She rolls her eyes then heads for the kitchen to get the twins something to eat.

As she was getting breakfast ready Bela walks in. ¡Um algo huele bien! "It does smell good grandma! I'm so hungry!" Joey says. "Me too!" Maribel yells. "Go wash up, put on the clothes I picked out, and come back to eat." The twins run to their room pushing one another to see who can get to the bathroom first. "Be good now ya'll! Stop pushing each other!" "Sam, they been doing that for 5 years now. You are the only one who could keep them under control." Spirit and Bela laughs. Spirit yells; "The Sherriff's back in town! No more pushing each other!"

Spirit calls Sara back. "You ready?" "Let me get the apps. By the way, you have siblings?" Spirit was silent for a few minutes. "Are you still there?" "Yup. I told you my business is my business." "I've been knowing you for over 3 years now and I really don't know anything about you! But you know all about me!" "Okay! OK! ¡Ah Dios mío! Sara! How much do you want to know!" "Let's start with where you at! Then you can go from there." "I guess you don't want them applications filled out huh?" "Nope! This more important!" Spirit takes a big breath and say; "You already know me as Spirit. My birth name is, Samantha Garcia. I'm from San Juan Puerto Rico. I have two brothers and one sister. The oldest his name is Emmanuel Jr. The twins' names are Joey and Maribel. We all belong to Emmanuel Sr. My grandparents live with us, they are Samuel & Marie Sanchez. OK! That's it!" "You didn't mention about your mother and how you ended up here in North Carolina!" "I gotta tend to the twins now. We talk later." Spirit closes her phone while Sara was still asking questions. She puts her phone on silent. The twins run in the house and yells; "Here come Manny!" Spirit laughs as she grabs the twins and starts ticking them. She looks up and there's Manny. She stands up and says; "¡Hola! ¿Que tal?" "Nada Mija." "You want sumthin' to eat?" "Naw. I'm good. Um why you speaking to me like we are handling business or somthin?" "What you mean?" she says as she goes into the kitchen to get dinner started. "Come here, sit down Sam!" "Please call me Spirit! That's my name before I left, and still is." "OK! You don't have to get testy! You ain't been around in so long, I forgot! Don't kill me!" Manny says as he puts his arms up over his face as if to protect himself. "Manny that's not funny."

"I came to let you know I ain't mad at chu anymore." "Who cares!" Spirit says. "Why did you change your name anyways?" "I told you before. I'm not now! Don't ask me anymore!" Spirit says with her arms folded as she leans to the side with her hip out. Manny reaches in his pocket and pulls out a one-hundred-dollar bill nice and new. Spirit looks at him with a smirk on her face. She leans toward Manny and say. "You can keep it. I don't need nor want it!" "So, you too good for my money, huh?" Spirit walks to the other room and comes back in 30 seconds with $300 in her hand. "See! I have money! Thank you tho!" "You can give me one of those then." He says as he reaches out to grab one. "I don't think so! Go get your own!" She leaves the room while Manny was laughing. Manny walks behind her. Spirit puts the money in her pocket, so Manny wouldn't see where she got it from. The twins run in yelling; "I want some money! Give it me!" they both say in unison. Spirit turns toward them and say. "You will get some when ya'll turn 18 for college or sumthin'" "Joey stops abruptly because Big Manny walks into the room. "Hey Pop!" says Manny Jr. "How you doing? How was work?" Big Manny asks. "Productive." What you know about that?" "Running my own business is productive." "What business you have now son?" "I market different stuff for tourists." "Isn't that seasonal?" "Yea but. I keep the money for my next venture. I'm coming to say goodbye anyways. The season is over with, so I'm heading off to "The States" to try it there." Spirit's eyes get big.

"Where you gone stay?" Spirit asks Manny Jr. "Don't you have a place there? I figured since you are here I can crash at Yo place. Huh? Unless you gave it up!" "Um yes and no." Spirit says. "What you mean by that!" Big Manny asks. "Yeah, either you do, or you don't!" Manny Jr. says as he leans forward with his hand by his ear as if to say what did you say. "Can we all sit down for a minute? Spirit says with her hand out towards the couch. I can explain." Big Manny asks; "What you been doing all these years in the states?" Spirit takes a deeper breath than she did talking to Sara. "Well, how can I say this? I'm homeless! It's been that way since I moved there!" They all said; "What you mean!" So loud that Belo and Bela come rushing into the living room. "What's going on!" Bela asks. "What is all this about?" "Sam just told us she been homeless for 5 years in the states!" Manny Jr. yells. "Is that true Sam?" Belo asks. Spirit nervously say; "Why ya'll jumpin on me fo!" ¡No, me gusta este!" Spirit runs to the bathroom and slams the door. She was so angry that tears start rolling down her face. "Come outa there Samantha we didn't mean to upset you." Manny Sr. whispers to Spirit threw the bathroom door. Disculpe por favor. Big Manny puts his hand on the door. Spirit slowly opens the door to grab her father around the waist real tight. She buries her face in his chest. Spirit was embarrassed because of what her and Gennie talked about 6 months ago, she knew this time would come but not like this. It was not a topic for the whole family to discuss as a group. Besides the subject never came up. Big Manny takes her to the couch to sit down as did the rest of the family. The food was cooking slowly on the stove. Bela went to make sure all was well in the kitchen. "Well Sam!" Manny Jr. yells at her. "Let her talk! ¡Cállate! Jr! Says Belo. Spirit lifts her head off her father's chest she looks up at him to say. "I-I've been living at this shelter." "A shelter!" Manny Jr. yells. ¿No dije que se callara? Emmanuel! Belo says. ¡Deja que termine de hablar! Sr. says. "Wait let me explain! I own the shelter with a friend and business partner. We met when I got to The States. She ran away from home at 17. Her father didn't protect her from his new wife. We have quite a few things in common. She looks at Jr. I was still sad and lost over mommy. I couldn't take it any more living here with people accusing me of stealing all that money when mom gave it to me. She told me not to tell anyone where I got it. "Jr. laughs at Spirit. She turns her head to the side in a look of confusion. "What's so funny?" "All that time you let people think you stole all that money? ¡La chica esta loca! We all know momma gave you that money!" For the first time in years Spirit let everyone see her cry. Everyone gets up. Jr. holds his hand out to her to help her up. They all surrounds her to give her a hug. "Thank you!" Spirit says. "Mom left all of us money! I mean dad and mom. They always had money they didn't live like it. I guess you the same way huh Mija? Living in a shelter." I told you I own it! I stay there to look to see if I can assist ones who may need some help. This little girl name Sara came along. She was 13 or so. She ran away from

Back To The Beginning

"How time flies" Joey says. "It's been so wonderful you being here and all Spirit." "Are you putting me out Joey?" Spirit asks jokingly. "Naw! I was hoping that you're going back to the states." "What you got up your sleeve Joey?" "Nothin. Sorry sis gotta take this call." Joey rushes out of the house. Spirit sits there on the couch looking at the door thinking yup how time does fly. That boy is so big." Sr. comes out of his room and sits next to Spirit. "Spirit I have something I need to tell you." "Yes Popi!"

She says as she shifts her body towards him. "I've met someone." "You have!" It's been over 14 years. Oh, that's why you barely been here or leaving so fast. I'm fine with it. Am I always last to know anything around here?" Joey comes in the house and immediately responds to that question. "Yup! Caz, you been doing Yo own thang around here." Where's your sister?" She's over her friend's house." "What friend?" "You know Cielo Martinez." "Wait! Don't she have a brother called Mateo?" Spirit asks. "Yup!" Spirit stands up and puts her hands on her hips. "What's going on? Who is she going over there to see? Mateo or Cielo?" Joey hesitates to answer. "Ambos especialmente Mateo and me Cielo." Spirit was still standing there with one hand on her hip. "We almost 16! We old enough to meet and like the other sex!" Spirit laughs at him. "You so proper with it, we're old enough to meet the opposite sex." She mocks him. "Okay Sam." Joey says sarcastically. "What you call me!" Spirit yells to Joey as she runs after him. Joey quickly runs out the door laughing. "Go get your sister! It's getting late!" Spirit yells again this time in the hallway of the apartment building. Joey yells back. "It's a Friday night! We'll be home by 11:00! Like every Friday!" "Be safe!" Spirit starts to yell but the building door had already slammed before she could finish saying it to him. "Popi, it's you and me now." "No Mija. I'm about to go to work." Sr. kisses Spirit on the forehead, grabs his things, and out the door he goes. Spirit sits back on the couch to enjoy her cup of tea.

Spirit starts thinking to herself. I been doing so much for everyone else. I wonder, what should I do next? She jumps up, goes to get her carrying bag and says out loud. "Time for me to make a visit to the states." She calls Gennie first and then Sara to tell them the good news. She tells Sara. "I'll see you in a few days." "I'm not going anywhere. I got all this school work to do. One more year then I'll have my master's in psychology. I've already signed up for an Internship on my own to get experience." She was packing and talking. "Good how are your parents?" "They fine enjoying each other's company as usual." "That's good. Well I'm about to finish packing and get some rest." "It's Friday night! Yells Sara. You about to go to bed Spirit! I gotta lot of homework. Sighs Sara. "I'm going crazy! I'm gone have to treat myself for that issue!" They both laughs. "Well Spirit you be safe." "See you when I get there." "Love you Spirit, can't wait so see you!" "Love you too Sara." Then Spirit pushes the end button on her phone while she stands there with a smile on her face. Then she starts humming as she packs her clothes for travel.

The next day everyone was up and getting ready to start their day. Spirit asks everyone to come take a seat in the living room where she was already seated. She pats the seat next to her for Maribel to sit next to her. Spirit starts to speak. "Well everyone. I'm going back to Charlotte for a little while. I've been gone for quite some time now. My business partner and friend Gennie have a family now. Sara is doing what she loves. As for me well, I need to see what I want to do for me now. Everyone here has someone to love but me..." "We love you Spirit!" Maribel says as she reaches over to grab Spirit's hand. Everyone agreed. "I know that! You all know what I mean. I want to get married, have children, to find out how it feels to be in an intimate relationship with someone who want to love me the same way I want to love him. I want purpose in life. Last night I realized how empty my life is. All of you have someone to care for and vice versa. I have no one to call and say I'm coming home I miss you! Spirit starts to get a little teary eyed, but she holds back by saying; "I've earned it and I deserve it!" Belo says with conviction."

¡Estoy de acuerdo! Everyone agrees but Maribel. Maribel yells; "Why can't you do that here! What am I going to do when you're gone!" "You can do something!" Spirit says as she caresses Maribel's hair. You're going to finish high school, go to college, career, get married and have a family to care for etc. I'm coming back Maribel. I'll call you every day. If time permits, you can come to the states and help me with the shelter and other things. In the meantime, I must get back to it. ¿Entiendes, verdad Maribel? Do you?" Maribel holds her head up proudly, looks at Spirit with tears running down her cheeks. Spirit grabs Maribel by the head to lay her head on her shoulder. "Aw Mijita esta bien. SHHH don't cry. I'll never forget about you. I'll call you every day. I promise. Will you do the same and when I do call answer my calls?" Maribel was still crying. "I will call you. I will." Spirit starts to wipe Maribel's tears away. Bela yells. "¡La comida está lista, ven a comer!" Everybody went to clean up except Maribel and Spirit. She was making sure Maribel is fine. They both gets up and Spirit grabs Maribel by the hand, they both goes to wash their hands to eat. Everybody stays in the house spending time with one another. Especially since Spirit is leaving. "Tell us about your friends! Especially the one you have the business with. Maribel asks. "I told you about Sara. She's doing her internship for her career as an adult and youth counselor. She said that I am her inspiration in how I helped her through those tough years." What did you do for her Spirit?" "She was homeless. I made sure that she was safe because her parents put an award out for her of $25,000. We were in another city. People were looking at her for bait to get the money and not interested in her well-being." Did you get the money Spirit?" "I did. I gave it to the shelter to get supplies and other necessities it needed." "Man, I wouda kept that money!" Joey says as he sits on the edge of his seat rubbing his hands together. "What happened next Spirit?" Maribel asks. "I looked after her for about 2 years." "She was homeless for that long!" "Yup! until I convinced her to call her parents and go home. She never slept on the streets. I always made sure that she had a bed to sleep in. I would be there with her until she fell asleep. She never knew that I am co-owner of the shelter. I would go to my place and be back before she woke up. A lot of people know me. They don't know that I am one of the owners of the shelter. I am a silent partner so to speak." Spirit laughs. "Like an assistant for Gennie. I went to live with Sara and her parents for about a year or so." "Why!" yells Maribel with a frown on her face. "Well... Sara wouldn't stay if I didn't stay. She didn't trust her parents since they didn't tell her that her older sister died. They lied to her for such a long time. Until her friend Elonda went missing. Actually... They thought I lived there with them. When they all fell asleep. I'd go back to my place. When they woke up I'd be sitting on the porch waiting for someone to come out." Why did you leave her, Spirit?" Joey asks. "Well... That's when I started to miss ya'll. She and her mom were close, and Sara was opening to her mom about her feelings. That whole three years or so wore me out I was exalted and now here I am." "Can I ask you another question Spirit? "Sure dear." "Why do you always leave places after being there maybe 3 to 5 years?" "Well Mija, it depends if my goals or should I say mission is complete." "Is your mission done here?" Maribel asks Spirit with a concerned frown on her face. Spirit grabs Maribel by the chin and says softly. "Mijita, my mission is never done here. This is my home, our home. Please don't change the locks!" Everyone starts laughing.

There was a knock at the door. Joey goes to open it. A tall thin woman walks in with long curly locks and ice gray eyes as if she could see though a person. Spirit stands up to stare at as if she's seen this woman before. "Have we met before?" Spirit asks. She says, "I don't know. I've been dating Emanuel for some time now." Spirit looks at her father. He gets up and walks toward the woman. "Sam. I mean Spirit. I want you to meet Carisa Gomez. My fiancé." Sr. tells Spirit as he kisses Carisa gently on the cheek. Spirit shakes her head as if she was shaking off a trans or blackout. "How are you? It is nice to meet you." "Igualmente." Carisa says as she held her hand out to Spirit. "You are beautiful." Spirit says as she shakes Carisa's hand. "Why have you been hiding her!" Spirit says loudly to her father. Sr. Laughs nervously as he says to Spirit; "Well Mija, I didn't want to upset you. I had to find a good time to introduce you to her. Since you are about to leave, now is the time." Spirit grabs Carisa by the hand to pull her to the couch with the family. She questions Carisa in interrogation style. After all was said and done. Spirit says in a commanding voice; "This is a very special man to us. Please don't break his heart." Spirit gets up and goes to the bathroom. She stands there staring into the mirror trying her best not to cry. One tear got away from her. Spirit has feelings of betrayal of her mom for accepting Carisa. Spirit walks back out there. "Well everyone I'm about to turn in." She hugs everyone even Carisa. Spirit nervously whispers in Carisa's ear. "Nice to meet you. Welcome to our family. ¡Buenas noches!

Good night! Love ya'll." Spirit disappears into another room. The next day everyone goes to take Spirit to the Airport. They all say their see you later with kisses, hugs, and tears. "Come back soon!" Spirit smiles at them and say; "If you don't come up there first!" She winks her eye at Maribel. Maribel stands tall with a smile on her face waving at Spirit as she disappears into the boarding hallway.

The flight was pleasant. Spirit was happy to get back to the States. She feels refreshed and ready to get to work. Gennie and her family meets her at the airport. They all gives hugs as Gennie introduces Spirit to her family. "You have a nice family Gennie. My time will come someday." Spirit says giggling. Gennie hugs Spirit again and say; "You will." They leave the airport and goes to Gennie's house. "Are you hungry Spirit?" "Yes! I am starving!" Gennie heads to the kitchen and Spirit follows. "Gennie, I hope you don't mind I invited someone over to meet you and your family. She'll be coming over later. It's that girl I helped in the past and she want to come see me. Since I'm going to be here a few days I thought this would be a good time for ya'll to meet." "No problem! A good friend of yours is a good friend of mine. I can't wait to meet this little girl who took all your time up and made you abandon me and the business." Gennie says laughing. Spirit has this serious look on her face.

The next day no one had any plans or business to attend to. They all sits around playing games and catching up. The doorbell rings. Eric jumps up. "I got it ya'll keep playin." "Hello. Is Spirit here she invited me over. She said that I could come visit her here." "No problem! Cummo in." Eric says with a sweeping motion of his hand. Gennie was in the baby's room checking on him. Spirit gets up walks to Sara. Sara starts walking briskly to Spirit and grabs her with tears of joy in her eyes. Eric slips out the room to attend to Eric Jr. with Gennie to give Spirit and Sara a moment to themselves. Spirit guides Sara into a room where they were last night. "Thank you Spirit for all you have done for me." "Little girl how many times you gone tell me that and how many times do I have to tell you it was all your doing, not mine! ¡Cabeza a cabeza!" They both start laughing. "What are you both laughing about without me?" Gennie says as she walks into the sitting area. Sara's back was towards Gennie. "Sara, I want you to meet my friend and business partner. Gennie Murphy." Sara stands turns around with a nervous smile on her face. Sara and Gennie stood there staring at one another. They both starts to cry and runs towards one another. Spirit stands there with her mouth open pondering about, what just happened. Spirit joins in the hugging so she won't be left out. She was still pondering. "You remember me telling you about my friend and sister, Lala? This is her!" Sara says excitingly. Lala where you been!!!"

Sara starts crying again. "I missed you so much! I've been worrying about you!" Gennie grabs Sara by the hand and pulls her down next to her on the couch. "I always had it pretty rough but after leaving your school things started going downhill more than ever. I used school and extra activities to keep my mind occupied off what was going on at home."

"What was going on?" "My dad got remarried without telling me and she didn't like me because I had most of my dad's attention. Especially after I told my dad about what was going on. She called me a liar and dad didn't do anything. My mom left me a lot of money to live on my own when I turn 18. I had this guy to help me to escape from it all. I was ready to live on my own. The last time I saw my dad was when I left that city and never looked back! Gennie says with tears in her eyes. "My dad told me that he would always protect me from the cruelness of this world because of my Albinism. He brought it into our own home when he married her without me knowing. He forgot to protect me from her and all day every day when he was not around she would so callously tell me how this world views people like myself. No one else ever made me feel ugly, worthless, unwanted, and self-conscious like she did. I didn't think of how I looked until he brought this woman into our lives." Gennie tells Sara with tears in her eyes. "Why did you change your name Lala?" Sara asks. "So, he would not be able to look for or find me." "How did you and Spirit meet?" "Sara my birth name is Samantha." "I changed it. Spirit and I met on common grounds, both our mothers died. They left us money. We met while we were both homeless about 9 years ago, we had each other's back. In turn we both wanted the same things. For people to have a decent place to sleep while they got themselves together. Along with assistance in accomplishing that. That is how the shelter and other programs started. For people like ourselves whom are different can have support and know that they are loved." "Something like AA only without the drugs and alcohol." Spirit says with a grin one her face. Unless someone has that issue and they would get other services along with our support group. "This is something we are so passionate about. Gennie says as she looks at Spirit. "That brings us to this day." "Um... Lala have you ever thought about me?" "Yes and no." Sara looks at Elonda with a confused look on her face. "I say no because I couldn't worry about something I don't have control over. I leave that to the Professionals." "Who is that!" You hired someone while I was gone!" Spirit says loudly. "NO!! It's Spirit." "What!" No not you! I mean He is a spirit not you Spirit." They laugh.

"Oh... Ok. I left that behind so many years ago." Spirit says. "Me too says Sara. "You guys are missing out! Tell me. How did we survive all we've been through! To be in this moment right here?" Elonda asks. "We are special and unique which singles us out. Everybody is special and unique, but some don't know that and never had anyone to tell them. I may be Albino. Sara with your fire red hair and crystal green eyes, like big marbles. Looking like you will burn up stuff. They all laughs. Samantha. With your black curly locks with silver streaks in odd places and silver eyes like you can see right through everyone. You scared me when we first met! Yells Elonda. "Me too!" yells Sara. They laugh so hard and loud Sara fell on her back to the floor.

Eric comes running out of the baby room. "Hey ya'll gone wake up JR!" "Sorry Honey!" Elonda with a low voice. We all got made fun of in one way or another. That does not take away our purpose, value, and uniqueness. Sara and Spirit sits there listening to Elonda talk about her faith and convictions.

A few months passes by and all the business ventures has been caught up. Sara is now the counselor. Spirit is still helping young lost ones to find their way. Elonda(Gennie) still holds it down with her silent partners so to speak. Her husband Eric, JR, and her God. Building up her faith. Trying to help Spirit and Sara build their faith. Sara has a lot of curiosity about it but Elonda is still working on Spirit in that department.

The girls have grown and matured. Elonda is 29 and still prefers to be called Gennie. Sara is now 25. Spirit is now 32 and wants to be loved by a special man. She may have found him.

Our lives have purpose! The roads we travel along the way could lead us to that very place. Through heartache, differences, faith, companionship, and support. We don't have to travel them alone. The destination is contentment, happiness, and love for ourselves and others.

Count Your Losses

Loss helps us to become meek.
Yes! Loss is a bad thing to go through.
We should remember others are losing too.
Loss can be experienced alone or with someone you love.
You are never alone.
The One with you is from Above.
Loss can be a transition to a new beginning.
Not always something that happened to you for sinning.
We all lose, that is a fact of life we go through.
Just wait you will figure out what to do.
Life goes on in the loss we are experiencing right now.
When it is over. Congratulate and take a bow.
Let us count our losses and messes.
If we didn't have them how could we appreciate our blessings!
GYC ©2007

Printed in the United States
By Bookmasters